MAGNUS

ROCK HARD MOUNTAIN MEN

BOOK ONE

BY EVIE RILEY

Magnus

Rock Hard Mountain Men

Book One

Copyright © 2025

Evie Riley

ISBN: 978-1-77357-747-0

978-1-77357-748-7

Published by Naughty Nights Press LLC

Cover Art By CDG Cover Designs

CHAPTER ONE

Magnus

I NEVER EVEN saw the fist before it collided with my jaw. It was only instinct that had me shifting my weight at the same time I felt contact with my skin, moving with the force of the blow so it didn't put me completely on my ass. As a South Paw, I was usually good at defending my left side, but some opponents adapted quicker than others and were able to slip past my guard.

This was, unfortunately, one of those

times.

My shoulder hit the bars that stood at my back, but I didn't let it stop me. Blocking out the pain as I'd learned to do long ago, I ducked under the man's next swing and landed my own hit right to the soft spot just under his ribs.

I heard him gasp as the air was knocked from his lungs while at the same time shooting a straight jab at his head. The man managed to dodge quick enough that my punch never landed, but it put enough space between us for me to catch my breath.

With the back of my hand, I wiped away the liquid dripping from the corner of my mouth, not bothering to look if it was saliva or blood.

Probably a mix of both.

A few feet away, my opponent stared me down, breathing just as heavily as me, and sporting several cuts and bruises, most of which I'd put there myself.

MAGNUS

He was getting tired. I could end this soon if I acted quickly enough. Although my own body ached, I kept my guard up as I charged forward, already envisioning exactly where I planned to hit him.

Somewhere off to the side, a bell rang. My opponent and I immediately dropped our hands and stood up straight.

"And at the end of the second round, both our challengers are still standing," the announcer called over the speaker. "With a tied score and one round left to go, who will come out on top? There's still time to place your bets, people."

I returned to my corner of the ring and reached through the surrounding bars to grab a water bottle and a towel. The break wouldn't last long, and I needed to gather as much strength as possible if I wanted to win the fight.

Underground cage fighting couldn't be called a real job, but it helped make ends meet on the months when my military pension just wasn't enough.

The lively crowd was a dark squirming mass just outside my vision. I couldn't see anything beyond the brightly lit cage. Occasionally, a few words trickled through to me, mostly curses, but I paid no mind to any of them. As I took another deep drink from my water bottle, my gaze stayed locked on my opponent across the ring.

I didn't remember his name. Jason? Johnson? Whatever it was, he was a tougher opponent than usual. We were equal in size, which wasn't surprising. Most of the men brave enough to get in this ring had plenty of muscle, but they often lacked the speed to back it up.

This latest opponent—Justin?—had both strength and speed in spades. Plus, he was younger than me by at least a decade. Ten less years' worth of old injuries acting up, and general wear and tear on the body. If it came down to a contest of endurance, he'd win.

But younger also meant he had ten less years' of experience. He didn't know how to hide his weaknesses well enough.

As I watched him wiping the sweat and blood from his face, I noticed the way he was standing. His weight was shifted just a little more onto one leg than the other. Since he hadn't been favoring his right leg earlier, I assumed he must have strained something when dodging my last punch.

I could work with that.

The break ended and the next round started. If I had my way, it would be the last one.

The two of us stood at the center of the ring, guards up, waiting for the signal to start. When the bell rang, I stepped to the side, forcing my opponent to turn to keep me in sight. He was surprised for a moment when I didn't immediately attack, but he wasn't left off balance for long. He swung for me, and I dodged just like last time. There was an opening for me to get a hit on his body, and it was tempting to take, but I held back.

I moved around him, never letting us stay in one place for long.

He swung for me again, and this time I blocked it instead. The clash of muscle and bone caused me to grit my teeth against the pain, but I held steady. I could have dodged, but that would have put me on the wrong side of him. I wanted to keep his weight on his bad leg and force him to use it as much as possible.

I could see in his eyes the moment he realized what I was doing. He tried to reposition himself so he could put more weight on his good leg, but I pressed forward, forcing him backward to avoid eating my fist.

When he stepped back, his balance jolted for a moment as his leg struggled to support him.

Almost.

MAGNUS

Cage fighting didn't have as many rules as regular fights. So long as we stayed inside the cage, didn't kill each other, and listened to the ref, anything went.

Because of my size—and let's face it, my age—most people assumed I lacked agility. While I wasn't as flexible as I had been in my youth, I wasn't out to pasture yet and still had a few impressive tricks up my sleeve.

I dropped my guard just enough that his next swing nearly landed. It took everything I had just to protect my face, and it gave him the opportunity to get his feet under him properly and finally give his bad leg a break.

A smug look spread across his face when it seemed like he'd broken free of my trap.

Then, faster than a blink, I dropped low to the ground and sung my body in a full circle to sweep out his legs. He stumbled back several steps, windmilling his arms to stay balanced. The sudden movement was too much for his leg, and it buckled.

He dropped to one knee at the same time I sprung up out of my crouch and threw my full body weight into an uppercut to his jaw. The combined forces of him falling directly into my punch sent him flying several feet. The metal bars around the ring clanged with a hollow echo when he hit them before his body slumped unconscious to the ground.

A moment of stunned silence passed as the crowd realized what had happened. Even the ref didn't respond right away, but after a pointed look from me, he started the countdown. A wave of noise, even louder than before, erupted from the crowd as they joined in on the count.

I stood to my side of the ring, tall and confident under the spotlight. While I kept one eye on my opponent, just in case they managed to get up, I already knew the match was over. My opponent didn't even twitch when the countdown hit zero. The crowd around me erupted. Some with joy and some with anger, depending on which way their bet had gone.

Based on a few furious faces, I would have to be careful when I went out to my car later. It wouldn't be the first time someone tried to jump me for daring to do my job and winning the fight.

The ref held up my hand, declaring me the winner as though it wasn't plainly obvious. Comically, the ref had to stand on tiptoe to raise my hand all the way up. Bright stage lights glinted off my bruised knuckles and the sweat that trickled down my arm. I would be so itchy later when my blood cooled and the sweat matted in the hair over my chest, but for right now, I felt so alive with euphoria it was as though I was standing on the top of the world.

EVIE RILEY

***

The drive from the old warehouse when the underground fights took place, and my home took about half an hour. Everyone knew about the fighting ring, but since it was so far outside of town, the local police didn't bother to worry about it. The only people who got hurt were the ones that agreed to it, so it wasn't worth the police's time. I was pretty sure I'd even seen a few cops in civilian clothes collecting their bets after the fight.

My own earnings for the night sat in the inner pocket of my jacket, all under the table cash that I would not be reporting in my taxes, thank you very much. The government already took plenty from my military pension. They didn't get to take this as well.

Just on the edge of town, a dirt road turned off from the main route, only noticeable to those who knew to look for it. My truck barely fit through the space between the trees, and branches clawed at the windows. There had been talk about widening the path, but the dense rustic nature of the forest had been one of the property's best selling points, so the trees stayed.

About a quarter mile, the path naturally widened out, revealing an open field with two RVs and several partially finished structures.

My retirement plan.

While in the military, I'd formed a close friendship with two of my brothers-in-arms, and we'd made a plan. Once we retired, we'd pool our money to buy a plot of land off in the mountains somewhere and live as off-grid as possible. Brody and I retired around the same time, so we'd gotten started on the project, but Creed still had a little time before he could leave. Plans for his part of the property were nothing but blueprints on paper, but they would come eventually.

Overall, it was still a work in progress, but it was progress none-the-less.

A patch of gravel along the side of the road acted as our communal parking spot. The moment I pulled my truck to a stop and opened the door, I could hear the repetitive banging of Brody hammering on something.

The aches and bruises from my latest fight had stiffened up on the car ride home, and my joints groaned as I climbed out of the truck and approached the newly built deck where Brody was nailing the last few planks into place.

During the day, Brody worked as a lumberjack, and he resembled his job description to an almost cliché level. Red hair, green eyes, big as a bear, and almost just as hairy as one. No one was surprised to learn he spent his days wielding axes and chainsaws. If anything, they were more surprised by his military history. He didn't look clean-cut enough.

I tugged at my long blond hair, which I kept tied back in a braid when I fought.

Then again, I didn't look clean-cut enough either. I'd started growing my hair out even before I retired from the military. It was technically a uniform violation, but at that point I was too good at my job and too near the end of my career for anyone to care.

Brody's hammer never stopped swinging, even when I stood only a few feet away.

"Mag," he called to me without looking up from his work. "How'd it go? You win?"

Pulling the wad of cash out of my pocket, I waved it at him.

"What's it look like? Now we can afford to re-pour the concrete foundation for the greenhouse.

There had already been a concrete slab at the edge of the field when we bought the place, left over from an old structure that used to be there. I'd been planning on utilizing it to build a greenhouse, but after closer inspection, I found the underground portions too eroded to support any weight. It would have to be redone, which was an extra expense we didn't have in the budget.

Finishing with the plank he was working on, Brody sat up and tossed the hammer aside.

"You know, the greenhouse could have waited. There's no reason to get started on it right away."

My gaze drifted over to the space where the greenhouse would someday stand. Right now, it was just a pile of supplies neatly packed away in boxes, but someday it would be a glorious structure of glass and plant life.

"Until I get the greenhouse going, we're limited to seasonal crops. The sooner the greenhouse is finished, the sooner I can start growing food for us all year long. I'm tired of spending so much money on groceries."

"True," Brody nodded. He picked up the last board and slotted it into place. It fit so well that it would stay even without nails, though of course it would be properly secured like everything else. Brody had a detailed eye for exact measurements. Give him some tools and an endless supply of wood, and he could build just about anything.

"I'm just about done here. You need help with anything?"

"Nah." I stuffed the cash back in my pocket. "I'm going to head into town and get the order placed for the concrete. We'll need more than the store probably carries on hand, so they'll need a few days to have it shipped in. May as well get it started as soon as possible."

Brody's hammer stopped mid-swing, comically poised just a few inches above a nail. He didn't even lower it when he glanced up at the sky.

"It's only, like, an hour and a half until sunset. You sure about going into town this late?"

"Yeah. I'll be fine. I won't be long."

"You better not be. I don't want you driving on those roads after dark. There are no streetlights out this far. You'll drive yourself right off a cliff."

"Thank you for your vote of confidence," I said as I stepped past him and headed inside the house.

"I'm just trying to keep your dumb ass alive," he called back to me. "And take a shower before you go. I've seen you come out of literal war zones cleaner than you are right now."

My only answer was a waved middle finger in his direction.

Though, he wasn't wrong. I really did need to shower before I exposed myself to civilized people.

The eventual plan was to have three fully built houses on the property. Brody's house was mostly finished, due to his carpentry diligence, whereas mine was little more than a foundation with a few walls. Most of my focus had been on the land, and getting our crops planted. So far, I'd managed to carve out a decent vegetable garden, a few fruit trees, and a chicken coop.

Luckily, Brody was willing to let me live inside his house until mine was finished as well. We had a couple RVs, which we'd lived in while first getting started, but nothing beat the convenience of an actual house.

With an actual properly sized shower. Bathrooms on an RV were not built for men of our stature.

My clothes were so stiff with dried sweat that they practically stood up on their own when I dumped them on the floor. The hot water from the shower was bliss on my stiff muscles, and I could have stood there for hours letting the shower pour down on me, but I needed to finish quickly. Brody's warning was no joke. Mountain roads could be treacherous at night, and I didn't want to be stuck driving home in the dark.

If I was smart, I'd wait and just go into town tomorrow, but...

...well, I'd never claimed to be smart.

The one thing I did take my time with was blow-drying my hair after the shower so I could let it hang free instead of keeping it tied back. Like this, it reached past my shoulders, creating a dark blond mane around my head. It was an impressive sight, if I did say so myself, and I enjoyed it despite the extra work it cost me.

Throwing on an unstained pair of jeans and a T-shirt, and the cleanest pair of boots I could find, I was back in my truck within fifteen minutes of arriving.

MAGNUS

From there it was a twenty-minute drive into town. That would leave me half an hour to finish up at the hardware store and get back on the road if I wanted to return home before sunset.

Plenty of time.

***

Emberwood was an old town with a lot of new buildings.

Well, new compared to the original age of the town. It was a pre-civil war settlement that should have been an impressive historical landmark. However, at around the turn of the twentieth century a fire swept through the town and burned a significant amount of it down. Most of the people had managed to get out before the fire spread, so there weren't many casualties, but not a single building had escaped unscathed.

Driving down the town's main road, there were still obvious signs of fire damage on some of the buildings. One would think they would be fixed after so long, but now, the burnt wood was put on prominent display.

The date of the fire was considered a local holiday. Apparently, the mayor of the town back then had been a particularly corrupt individual. If even half the stories about him were true, then he was a villain straight out of a children's fable. Due to his own arrogance, he'd ignored the early warning signs about the fire, and had ended up as one of the few victims of the flames.

Killed by his own hubris.

Once he was gone, the town was free to prosper. It had been renamed Emberwood in memory of the fire that had saved it, and any evidence of the fire was displayed like a badge of honor.

Inside the hardware store was mostly empty, with only a few last minute shoppers loitering around.

MAGNUS

I headed for the service desk located at the back of the store, internally crossing my fingers that I had timed things right.

Standing behind the desk was a man with chestnut brown hair and kind eyes. The tag on his uniform read Carlton.

His family owned the town's only hardware store, the only florist, and the only bank. He bounced between these three shops, so his schedule was hard to pin down. Because of this, I'd only managed to speak with him a few times, and no more than a few sentences in total.

My palms already felt sweaty, and I wiped them on my pants.

For most of my military career, there had been a strict Don't Ask Don't Tell policy, so I'd never been free to explore, or even really think about my sexuality. Once the policy had been lifted, there hadn't been any reason to bring it up, and I'd gotten so used to keeping that part of myself under lock and key that I maintained the habit right up until my retirement.

But it was different now. I was just an ordinary citizen, and more importantly, the state I lived in now had plenty of discrimination laws to protect the gay community.

LGBT community?

I wasn't very well versed in the appropriate terminology for these things, but I thought that's how it was referred to now. More inclusive than just gay.

There was literally nothing stopping me from marching over to the desk and asking the man out. Even if he said "no" so what? My life would go on. I was already certain Brody and Creed wouldn't care.

We'd never really talked about it, but the reason we'd all initially bonded was because we had the same secret to keep. Creed was still pretty deep in the closet and had only just recently opened up to the idea of being bisexual, but we all knew even if we never voiced it out loud.

Yep. There was nothing stopping me. Except myself. No matter how many times I recited the same mantra of encouragement in my head, I couldn't convince myself to cross the last few feet and approach the counter.

The decision was eventually made for me when Carlton looked up and spotted me.

"Mister McGuire. Back again? What can I get for you this time?"

"Ah, um..." I coughed awkwardly to try and relieve the sudden dryness of my throat and approached the desk. "I need to order some concrete. I know it's late, but I'd like to get started on the project as soon as possible."

I described what I needed, falling back on the comfortable formality of easily defined numbers.

Carlton checked their inventory on the store's old computer and frowned at the screen. "I'm afraid we don't have that much on hand. I can give you about a third of it right now, but the rest we'll have to order in."

"That's fine." I leaned my hip against the counter and nearly knocked over the candy display by the register. I managed to catch it before it fell, but a few Snickers bars still clattered to the floor. "Uh... heh. Sorry. I mean, a third is more than enough for me to get started. I'll take it now and pick up the rest later."

After arranging the details of the order, I counted out the bills from my recent earnings to pay for it. Carlton didn't ask any questions or hesitate to accept the payment as I handed over hundreds of dollars in cash. It wasn't the first time I'd paid in such a way, and the good thing about small towns was that people knew when to get nosey and when to keep their questions to themselves.

There were only a few minutes left before the store closed, so Carlton helped me haul the bags of concrete I was taking home today into my truck. The bags were at least eighty pounds each, and I couldn't help but watch how the muscles in Carlton's arms strained as he hauled around the heavy weight.

At one point, he threw one of the bags over his shoulder, causing his shirt to ride up enough to show off the curve of his stomach, and I forgot everything I was doing. My brain short-circuited, as if my thoughts had been replaced by white static, and the bag of concrete I was carrying slipped from my arms.

It hit the ground with a loud thud and burst open, spilling gray concrete powder everywhere.

For a moment, I just stared at the mess lying at my feet, not saying a word as I processed what I was looking at.

"Opps," Carlton called as he deposited another bag onto the back of my truck. "Careful. They're heavier than they look."

I pointed toward the ruined bag as the back of my neck burned with embarrassment. "I can pay for that."

Carlton waved off my offer and picked up another bag. "Don't worry about it. Happens all the time. Why don't you let me get the rest? There should only be two more."

The last two bags were loaded into the truck without incident, and with one last confirmation about the rest of the order, I climbed into the driver's seat.

Long after Carlton had already gone back inside the store, I still sat there, steadily beating my head against the steering wheel.

"Stupid. Stupid. Stupid. Why do I even bother?"

For a few minutes, my embarrassment burned hot in my stomach, but eventually, it turned to cold resignation, and I turned the key to start the truck, reveling in the growl as the engine roared to life.

The drive back home felt simultaneously both longer and shorter than the drive into town. I wouldn't have been surprised to find that I'd been gone a week, but I fulfilled my promise to Brody and the last rays of sunlight were disappearing from the sky just as I pulled my truck into the gravel parking spot on our property.

The concrete stayed in the truck bed. I could deal with it in the morning. I meandered straight from the truck to the firepit behind Brody's house, where I found the man sitting in a folding chair with a beer in hand.

Without saying a word, I grabbed another beer from the cooler near his feet and collapsed into my own folding chair beside him.

I could feel his eyes on me, but he at least had the courtesy to wait until I'd chugged half the can in one go for speaking up.

"So... how'd it go with the handsome cashier?"

"Shut up." I scowled at the dancing flames within the firepit, not willing to look at Brody's knowing smirk.

"That bad, huh?"

The second half of the can was downed almost as quickly as the first and I tossed the empty aluminum into a waiting trash bag.

"I said, shut up."

Brody hissed between his teeth. "Ooooh. Worse than I thought."

I grabbed another beer from the cooler but didn't immediately chug this one, choosing to stare forlornly into the fire instead.

A black shadow moved in the outskirts of the firepit, and one of our dogs trotted into view. Onyx was a burly looking Rottweiler, missing one ear and with a few scars along his back from old fights. He was only a few years old, but when he flopped down at our feet in the dirt, he sighed like a retired senior citizen that had spent his entire life in the coal mines.

When we'd first bought the property, we intended to get one or two dogs to act as a guard. Instead, when we went to the shelter, we ended up bringing home three dogs.

A second dog followed Onyx a moment later and lay down next to him. Indigo was a Pitbull, a little shorter and stockier than Onyx but with the biggest smile on any dog I'd ever seen. So many people had walked away from him at the shelter due to being built like a little body builder, but when we saw him, he'd been sitting in his cage grinning from ear to ear as he waited for attention.

The two dogs lay down right under our

chairs, acting like oversized foot warmers, while Brody and I stared off into the darkness, waiting for the third member of the pack.

He appeared a moment later, slowly appearing in the firelight like he completely expected us to be waiting for him. Pip was a longhaired Chihuahua that wasn't even a foot tall and took four steps for every one step of the other dogs. His little nose stayed pointed to the sky as he pranced right past the others and headed over to the small dog bed raised up on a box to keep it out of the dirt. After spinning in a few circles, he sat down and looked directly at each of us, as if giving us permission to carry on with whatever we were doing.

After the dogs were settled, and only the sounds of the night remained around us, I cracked open the beer in my hand and waved it vaguely at Brody like a drunk orchestra conductor.

"Talk to me about something else. Anything else."

For a moment, it looked like Brody might press the issue, but then he changed his mind and tossed me his phone.

"I got a message from Creed earlier. He says he's got some contact with a startup company in Switzerland that's making a new kind of solar panel for greenhouses. It's still experimental, but apparently the panels can produce solar energy and help plants grow better in a greenhouse."

"Okay." I looked through the messages on Brody's phone and the information that Creed had sent. It seemed legitimate, but that still left a few questions. "Why are they willing to work with us? We're not a big corporation or anything?"

Brody shrugged and popped the tab on another beer. "They say it's easier to install them from the beginning rather than try to retrofit an already existing structure, plus they don't want to be controlled by a large corporation. However, there are surprisingly few private greenhouses being built that are large enough."

It was a good idea, assuming it wasn't a scam. Anything coming from Creed was probably legit, the man was too paranoid to be taken for a ride, but one could never be too careful. One thing I'd learned the hard way, when the chips were down, most people would take what they could get and run. I'd been lucky enough to find two people I could trust. I doubted I'd be lucky enough to find more.

A high sharp bark rang out across the field. Pip didn't even bother to stand up. His single bark was all he needed for Onyx and Indigo to jump to their feet, hackles up, and snarls on their faces.

Although I didn't see anything out in the dark, I grabbed the knife hanging in a holster from my chair.

Pip wasn't a fighter. I don't think the little thing had ever lifted a paw more than necessary, but he had a keen pair of eyes and a sixth sense for threats.

I scanned the darkness around us, looking for any sign of a disturbance. Up in the mountains, surrounded by trees with not a city light in sight, it wasn't as quiet as most people would think. The forest was always full of sounds, especially at night when so many creatures came out to play.

The trick was to know the dangerous sounds from the normal ones. Bullfrogs bellowed from a nearby pond, coyotes cackled in the distance, and the trees creaked and groaned in the wind. It was a constant symphony, and all completely normal.

Beside me, Brody stepped away just long enough to grab the gun hanging on a rack on the house's back porch.

"Could be a bear," he said as he lined

the scope up to his eye. "It's about the time of year for them."

At first glance, the gun didn't look like anything more than an ordinary rifle, until you looked closer at the hardware. A high-tech night vision scope had been mounted on the top, and the barrel was modified for greater accuracy.

In the military, Brody had been a successful sniper with more kills under his belt than he wanted to admit to.

Hand to hand combat had always been my specialty. We'd made a good team, with me getting up close to enemies while he covered my back. We were, however, one man short without Creed here, and it put us on edge.

"Not enough noise for a bear."

The moment stretched on without any disturbances as Brody and I had a standoff with the night. Eventually, the dogs calmed down and lowered their guard, so we figured it was probably safe, but we weren't able to relax after that. We called it a night, put out the fire, and went to bed early. Though, Brody and I each took turns in the early hours of the morning to double check all the locks on the house. Just to be sure.

***

The next morning, we found signs of some disturbed underbrush out in the trees and a few broken sticks, but no signs of any prints. Not even animal tracks. The ground was dry since it hadn't rained in a little while, so it wasn't the best conditions for tracking, but whatever it was must have been either small enough or careful enough not to leave evidence behind.

Without any more evidence, there wasn't much we could do, so we turned our attention to other matters. Brody had to leave for his shift with the logging company he worked for, so I decided to get started on fixing the concrete base for the greenhouse.

After last night's little trip into town, I had enough concrete mix to get started, but first I had to remove the old slab. I'd been hoping to save some of it to conserve materials, but as I poked around the corners of the concrete foundation buried in the ground, I found it beyond redemption. The concrete was older than I thought. Maybe even old enough to have been here before the fire that gave the town its name. It crumbled every time I touched it and wouldn't be able to support any weight.

A complete replacement was the only option.

With sledgehammer in hand, I started pounding away at the slab, breaking it into more manageable pieces for removal.

Onyx and Indigo were pacing the perimeter of the property, keeping an eye on things and paying special attention to the area where we'd found the disturbed underbrush. Meanwhile, Pip sat in his place of honor on a specially built ledge on his doghouse, watching over the chickens like a lord observing his vassals. Every now and then, Onyx and Indigo would come over to touch noses with their smallest pack member, before returning to their patrol rounds.

It was easy to imagine Pip as a little mob boss, commanding his much larger and stronger henchmen. Everyone was just his servant.

Even me.

When the sun was directly above us and I'd gotten most of the concrete slab broken up, Pip barked at me once to remind me it was lunchtime.

I took a break long enough to grab some water and a sandwich for myself and dump some food in the dog's bowls. I had to bring Pip's bowl out to him when he refused to come down from his perch, and I shook my head at him as I watched him eat one piece of kibble at a time.

"You are so spoiled. I wonder, did your previous owners give you up, or did you give them up?"

He stopped eating to glare up at me, sniffing and bobbing his head like he knew exactly what I was saying and was mocking me.

"Yeah, yeah." I picked up a shovel to get back to work. "You picked us, not the other way around. Got it. I'm so glad we meet your standards."

Most of the concrete could be removed with a shovel, but a few pieces were still too big and had to be hauled away by hand. It was as I was moving one of these larger pieces that I noticed something odd beneath the concrete. I mistook it for a tree root at first, but when I tried to break it up with the shovel, it echoed with a dull wooden sound, one that usually indicated something was hollow.

MAGNUS

Was something buried under the concrete?

Only a few inches of wood were exposed so I couldn't tell how big the thing was, but as I picked around with the shovel, I couldn't find the edge. More concrete had to be moved out of the way and the dirt beneath it removed to reveal the entire wooden object. It took me another hour to uncover the whole thing.

I stepped back, looking at what I'd found. The shape was unmistakable.

It was a coffin.

CHAPTER TWO

Trent

RUNNING AN ANTIQUE shop had not been part of my life plan. I'd had a lot of plans as a kid. Firefighter. Olympian. Superhero. An antique seller had not been anywhere on that list.

However, life had a way of making choices for us.

I'd spent my twenties and most of my thirties pursuing a career in competitive weightlifting. Even got good enough to place in a few international competitions.

Then, one wrong lift changed everything.

Now, with two bad knees, I spent most of my time sitting behind a desk waiting for customers to walk through my door.

It was a particularly slow day at the shop, not that an antique shop ever got that busy. Most of my business was done online, and the only reason I even kept the physical store open was the fact that the mortgage was already paid off. All I had to do was pay for utilities, which were covered by the few sales I made in person each month.

Plus, it gave me something to do rather than spend my days sitting around at home.

I was halfway through the book I was reading, reclining behind the desk with my feet propped up on the counter, when the bell over my front door rang. Not just once, but several times.

The book slipped from my hands and hit the floor when I found several members of law enforcement, along with a few people I didn't recognize, standing around my desk.

"Trent Earhart," the nearest man said, who seemed to be someone with authority.

"Yeah." The single word rolled slowly off my tongue, like each letter was its own sentence.

"We need you to come with us."

"Uh... why?"

The man scowled at me, seemingly unable to comprehend the fact that I wasn't immediately jumping to follow his command. He opened his mouth like he was about to issue another order, when the smaller woman at his side grabbed him by the ear and twisted hard.

"Stop barking at people," she said as the man flailed under her merciless fingers. "You scare everyone away as soon as you open your mouth. That's no way to talk to someone whose help we need."

She let the man go, and this time he kept his mouth shut as he rubbed at his ear and glared at her.

With a bright smile on her face, the woman turned to me.

"Hi. I'm Deputy Belrose. We need your help with a case that's just cropped up."

"Um…" To give myself time to think, I picked up the book from the floor and dusted it off. It was a sappy romance book, the kind usually targeted toward repressed soccer moms. I found them enjoyable, but I'd long since learned that reading such things publicly would get me ridiculed, so I'd swapped the cover with some generic war novel that I'd never actually read.

No one gave the book a second look as I set it on the counter in plain sight.

"I guess I'll help if I can, but I don't know what I can actually do for you. What's the case about?"

The man, whose name I never got, had

finally recovered from the abuse of his ear, and now stood beside Deputy Belrose with his arms crossed like he was trying to take up as much space as possible.

"A body was found up at old Milford's place."

"Old Milford's place?" I repeated, wracking my brain for anything I could remember about it.

Ben Milford was one of the last surviving descendants of the founder of our town. He'd died thirty years ago, and his property had gone up for sale since he had no living kin to inherit it. The land was mostly wild, and not good for much besides hunting, so it had sat vacant and unwanted for literal decades.

It had been referred to as Old Milford's place for so long that most people forgot the man wasn't still living there.

"Wait," I said when a memory returned to me. "Didn't someone just buy that place recently?"

The unnamed man scoffed. "Yeah. Some retired military guys from out of town who're trying to turn it into an off-grid farm or something."

He didn't need to say what he thought about this plan or these people. His expression said everything for him.

Luckily, Deputy Belrose interrupted him before he went on a proper rant.

"When the new owners were remodeling, they uncovered a body buried under the foundation of an old structure. We're investigating to figure out who it is and what happened."

"Okay." I flipped my thumb across the corner of my book, letting the edges of the paper that held the true hidden story rub against my skin. "That still doesn't explain what you need me for. I can't help you identify a body."

Deputy Belrose quickly shook her head. "No. We've got that covered. But there were a few objects found in the coffin that we were hoping you could help us analyze. None of our people know much about antiques. We could have them sent out, but I'd feel more comfortable trusting someone local."

What else was I supposed to do but agree?

When law enforcement asks for help, rejecting them isn't really an option.

"Sure. Just let me lock up the shop."

I stood from the desk and wasn't disappointed by the reaction I got. It was the same every time. When I was sitting down, I looked normal. It was only when I stood up that people were reminded of my past as a competitive weightlifter. Sure, I was softer around the middle than I used to be, but I still had plenty of muscle left.

Closing the place wasn't as easy as it seemed. With so many valuable objects all in one place, I had plenty of security measures and different locks that needed to be set in place. The whole process took about ten minutes. When I finally closed the front door behind me, most of the people had left, except for Deputy Belrose and the unnamed man.

The Deputy waited on the curb with a patient smile on her face, but the man was obviously much more impatient. He leaned against the wall of the building, angrily tapping his foot like he was counting the seconds as they passed.

His shoes were strange. The black patent leather looked classic and well taken care of, but the laces were bright white nylon, like the kind one would find on a pair of sneakers. My best guess was that the original strings had been damaged and he'd replaced them with the only thing on hand.

It was a small detail, but it revealed that the man was not as put together as he appeared. Such a little thing instantly relieved some of the tension I felt and put a smile on my face. Even such an intimidating person was just putting on a facade, like everyone else.

The car ride up to Old Milford's place was awkwardly silent as the two law enforcement officers sat in the front or the cop car, with the man behind the wheel. It turned out his name was Deputy Hillard, so I couldn't call him the unnamed man anymore, but having a name for him didn't make him any more likable. If anything, it only made him pricklier as he struggled to navigate the backroads.

I tried not to snicker as I rode in the back of the cop car like I was being arrested.

Did the man not drive much?

Everyone who lived in such an out-of-the-way town ended up driving on old backroads sooner or later.

Or maybe he was just a bad driver. All the experience in the world couldn't make up for a lack of skill.

The last time I'd been near this

property was when I was a kid, and I'd forgotten how tucked back in the trees it really was. We missed the turn off twice before finally finding the right path and following the dirt road up to the heart of the property.

With the bump of each tree root and the crunch of stones under the tires, Deputy Hillard grew more and more irate, until his face was so red it looked like it was about to pop right off his shoulders. I was relieved when the car finally came to a stop so I could get away from him as quickly as possible.

Half a dozen other cars waited for us on the property, parked haphazardly over the grass when the gravel parking spot couldn't accommodate everyone. I could see evidence of the work the new owners had put into the place. One new house was completely built, another was halfway finished, and based on the spacing it seemed like a third would probably be erected at some point. The land around each house had been cultivated, and an impressive garden stretched between them, complete with freshly tilled dirt, fruit trees along the edge, and a chicken coop on one side.

Behind the half-finished house, I could just see signs of broken concrete and dug up dirt. Most of the people were congregating around this area, and though I couldn't hear what they were saying, no one looked happy.

That must have been where the body was found. I didn't want to go anywhere near it, and to my relief, Deputy Belrose asked me to stay put.

"We've got the scene roped off right now, so it'll be easier if we just bring the items to you."

I was left waiting near the car with nothing to do with myself except kick my heels in the dirt.

That was when I noticed the other

person standing around far away from the chaos. I could tell he wasn't law enforcement, but it took me a minute to realize that this was probably the owner of the property.

When they said Old Milford's place had been bought by a couple of retired military veterans, I'd expected someone older, like my grandfather who'd also been a veteran. This man, however, was about the same age as me. Early forties at the most without a speck of gray in his long blond hair.

There was no way that hairstyle met uniform regulations. My grandfather had maintained the strict military style even after he retired, but this man had apparently gone the opposite direction. His clothing was stained with dirt and concrete dust, and several pieces of his sweat soaked hair had fallen out of a ponytail to hang around his face.

Two large dogs sat at his feet, alert but

calm as they watched the people invading their territory. The man's blue eyes were also pinned to the group of people stomping around his property and digging up his yard, and the twist of his mouth said he was not happy about any of it.

A healthy bruise darkened his jaw, standing out starkly against his pale skin. The sight of that bruise sparked a memory, and I realized I recognized the man. Just yesterday, I'd seen him win a cage fight.

Overcome with curiosity, I approached him.

"Hi," I said when I was close enough for him to hear me.

The man and the two dogs all turned to look at me in unison, and I stumbled back when one of them started growling. For a moment, I almost thought the man was growling at me, because the sound didn't come from either of the two dogs.

Then I noticed the third dog being

carried in his arms. The tiny little thing nearly fit in the palm of his hand, but its lips were pulled back into a ferocious snarl, and it growled so hard at me its whole body shook.

The man ran a hand over the little dog's head few times, soothing it. "Pip, stop that. You're fine. Sorry, he thinks he owns everything, and he gets territorial when his authority is challenged."

Realizing a little too late that the last part of the man's statement was directed at me, and not the dog, I laughed awkwardly to cover the silence.

"It's no problem. I wouldn't be happy with a bunch of strangers stomping around my home either."

Remembering my etiquette around new dogs, I held out the back of my hand for the little dog to sniff. At first, he continued to growl at me, but then he lowered his head just enough for his cold wet nose to touch my skin. This was apparently enough for him to decide I was harmless, for he stopped growling and settled back into his owner's arms. Even the two dogs sitting on the ground seemed to grow more relaxed, and I took it as a sign to come closer.

"That's better," the man said, though at first, I wasn't sure if he was talking to the dog or me. "See. Meeting new people isn't so bad."

He was talking to the dog, though in all honesty it could have still applied to me anyway.

The hand that wasn't holding a Chihuahua was stuck out toward me in the universal request for a handshake.

"Magnus McGuire. I'm one of the owners of this property."

"I figured as much," I said as I shook his hand. "Trent Earhart. I'm not entirely sure what I'm doing here."

After literal decades training at the gym to lift as much weight as possible, the strength of my grip usually startled people, but Magnus didn't even look like he noticed as he met my grip with equal strength.

"I saw you fight." The words tumbled out of my mouth without permission, and my face instantly burst into embarrassed flames.

Magnus's mouth twitched up into a smile, though I couldn't tell if it was sincere or not. "Excuse me?"

Since I was already babbling, I decided I might as well continue. There was no use hiding my awkwardness now.

"Yesterday. I saw you fight. You were really impressive."

"Hmm." He looked me up and down for a moment, and the heat that had been confined to my cheeks traveled along my whole body.

"You don't seem like the type."

He must have realized how he sounded because he immediately grimaced and sucked air though his teeth.

Apparently, I wasn't the only one prone to sticking my foot in my mouth.

"Sorry," he groaned, and pushed some of his flyaway hair out of his face. "I didn't mean... ah, fuck. I meant to say, I'm glad you liked the fight. It'd be real depressing if I was getting my ass beat, and it wasn't even entertaining."

"But you won."

"Doesn't mean I didn't get my ass beat. Just means the other got his beat even harder. No one comes out unscathed in a fight."

It was a joke, and we both laughed, but there was a thread of truth in his statement. I'd seen firsthand how conflicts claimed casualties on both sides.

'Winning' a fight often wasn't worth it in the end.

Before I could subject Magnus to any more of my terrible conversation skills, Deputy Belrose returned carrying a nondescript cardboard box.

"Mister Earhart. There you are. If you could just look at these things and tell us anything you notice about them, that would be a big help."

She handed me the box, which I brought over to the porch of the finished house so I could spread out the contents.

Inside the box lay three objects. A key, a locket, and an old leather-bound journal. My gaze went to the key first, as it didn't require careful handling. I picked it up, feeling the weight in my hands and observing the craftsmanship of the metal.

Deputy Belrose and Magnus watched me, patient at first, but Magnus quickly became restless. He reached out like he was about to take the key from my hands, but Deputy Belrose blocked him.

"Mister McGuire. Maybe it's best if you wait somewhere else for us to finish up. This really doesn't concern you."

"Doesn't concern me?" The Chihuahua

in his hands started growling again, this time directed at the Deputy. "These things were found inside a coffin buried on my property. Of course it concerns me."

"This key is old," I quickly said to head off the rising argument. Like, real old. Not the fake old you see on modern objects trying to look antique. The patina is natural rather than from artificial aging."

Deputy Belrose nearly reached for the key herself but restrained herself. "Can you be more specific?"

"Well, I can't tell you exactly when it was put in the ground, but I can tell you that it was originally made at least a hundred years ago. It's also a custom job. The end here doesn't match the usual design for keys at the time, so it must have been made for something very specific. Probably not a house, or anything common like that."

Relinquishing the key over to Deputy Belrose's hands, I picked up the locket next. It was a heavy piece, nearly the size of a plumb, and intricately carved in the image of a rose.

"This was probably made by the same person who made the key. The metalwork bears a similar style."

Despite its age, the clasp of the locket still held strong, proving the quality of the work. It took a little prying, but I managed to get it open. Inside, a picture had been lovingly framed, but it was too damaged by age and weather to see clearly. It was definitely a person. However, the face was nothing but a brown smudge.

Lastly, I picked up the journal, holding it very carefully in my hands. The leather was delicate after sitting abandoned for so long, and I feared it would disintegrate the moment I tried to open it.

"This needs to be handled in a more secure environment, but I can say that it was made by a different person than whoever made the locket and the key."

MAGNUS

Deputy Belrose carefully put the journal back inside the cardboard box. "How can you be certain? There's no name on any of it."

I pointed to the small metal charm decorating the strap that held the journal closed. It was also engraved with a rose.

"The style of the metalwork is different. Plus, whoever made the key and locket had a very steady hand to do that kind of detailed engraving. However, the engraving on the journal's charm is scratchier, and the handwriting inside the journal is jagged and chaotic. It's not the same person."

Nodding as she accepted this information, Deputy Belrose started putting the other objects in the box, but I stopped her.

"Actually, can I keep the locket? I may be able to restore the picture inside."

She considered the locket for a moment, but since it didn't seem as important as the key or the journal, she handed it over with little fuss.

"All right. We wouldn't be able to do much with it, and as I said, we'd rather not have to send it off somewhere. If you think you can restore it, then by all means, feel free to try."

She took the other two objects with her, leaving the heavy locket in my hands where it slowly absorbed the warmth of my skin. I carefully wrapped the jewelry in a soft, acid-free cloth and tucked it into my jacket pocket.

"That was impressive," Magnus said as he sat on the porch next to me. "How'd you know all that stuff from such a quick look?"

The Chihuahua he'd been carrying jumped down from his arms and decided that my lap looked like a better roost. It climbed up onto my legs and spun around a few times before curling into a ball and closing its eyes.

MAGNUS

When I shrugged, I tried to move as little as possible, so I didn't disturb the dog from its nap.

"I own an antique store. That kind of info is just stuff you pick up after spending time with old things long enough. It's no big deal. My grandmother probably could have told you even more."

The two larger dogs both rested their heads on Magnus's knees, and he stroked their heads with both hands at the same time. "It's still impressive. I don't know anything about any of that. Although, if you're going to be helping with this case, I should probably get your number. Deputy Belrose gave me a contact number for her, but I've got nothing for you, and it looks like it might be a while before this whole mystery gets solved. I may need your help in the future."

"Oh, yeah, sure," I said as I eagerly gave him my number, then handed over my phone so he could put his own number in as well.

It wasn't until he was handing my phone back with a new contact filled out that I realized what I'd done.

I'd just gotten a man's number. Sure, it was for work purposes, but it was still the farthest I'd gotten with a man for a while.

The chances of me calling him were slim, and he probably wasn't even gay, but the fact that I even had the confidence to exchange numbers with someone so handsome still filled me with a warm rush of confidence.

***

Later that night, I was working in the back room of the store as I tried to refurbish the picture from the locket.

The hardest part had been getting the paper out of the locket without tearing it. That alone had taken me several hours, and the sun had gone down long ago when I finally managed to get the paper isolated.

It wasn't in as bad of condition as it seemed at first. The picture had been protected by a glass pane, and much of the discoloration came from the aged glass. Removed from the locket, the picture was already more legible. Enough for me to tell it was a picture of a woman.

From there, I just had to carefully clean it up, using tools and chemicals specifically designed for such a use.

Old photo paper wasn't the same as modern day photographs and reacted very differently to certain abrasive chemicals.

Eventually, around midnight, I'd managed to get the picture as cleaned up as I could. The face in the photo stared up at me under the desk spotlight, as foreign and unknown as she'd been before she had a face.

I don't know what I expected. There was no reason for me to believe I would recognize the woman in the photograph even once I did get it cleaned up and legible. Yet, I still couldn't help feeling disappointed.

My contributions weren't going to solve the mystery. The information I'd told them probably wouldn't help at all.

What good would knowing that the same person made the key and the locket but not the journal actually do?

That didn't help reveal anyone's identity, and certainly didn't explain how a random body had ended up buried under a slab of concrete in Magnus's place.

I set my tools down, stripped off my nitrile gloves, and leaned back in my chair with a sigh.

I was a fool.

My pity party was interrupted when my security alarm went off. I reacted automatically, reaching for my phone to hit the emergency button.

MAGNUS

My grandmother had been a paranoid person in her old age and had installed an impressive security system in her shop. With just the press of a button, armored panels suddenly dropped over every door and window, barring the way in.

I tried to tell myself that it was probably just a petty thief, or some rowdy teenagers who thought vandalizing a local shop would be fun. It certainly wouldn't be the first time. Yet my stomach twisted with dread as I checked the security footage.

Someone dressed in all black stood outside the shop, banging against the armored panel with a crowbar. When that didn't work, they tossed the crowbar aside and fled.

The failed intruder was completely covered and dressed in all black. Even their eyes were barely visible, so there was nothing to identify them. However, as they ran down the street, just before they disappeared, a particular detail caught my eye and stole the air from my lungs.

The failed intruder wasn't entirely dressed in black. There, on their feet, white shoelaces stood out against the dark backdrop of their black leather shoes.

CHAPTER THREE

Magnus

THE SHRILL SOUND of my phone woke me from a deep sleep. I rolled over in bed, snatched my phone from the bedside table and stared at it ringing and vibrating in my hand. I cursed.

"Who the hell calls someone at six in the morning? Goddamn psychopaths, that's who."

As much as I wanted to just hit the ignore button, I didn't. It had to be important. I didn't give my personal number out to many people, and the few I did wouldn't call me so early on a whim.

Shaking myself awake properly and rubbing the lingering sleep from my eyes, I finger-punched the green icon and answered the phone.

"Hello?"

I was still too tired for full sentences, so the terse greeting would have to do. My voice barely sounded like me to my own ears, rough and deeper than normal as my vocal cords slowly remembered how to work again.

"Mister McGuire?" the voice on the other end of the line said. "This is Deputy Belrose. Sorry to call so early, but I need to ask you a few questions."

Deputy Belrose?

Right. Yesterday, I found a coffin buried on the property.

"Sure. Ask away, though I'm not sure what more I could tell you."

Her voice was clipped, almost on the

verge of being rude. "Did you notice any disturbances last night. Anything unusual, even something small."

"You mean aside from the coffin-shaped hole in my backyard?"

She didn't need to respond. Her silence made her opinion about my joke very clear.

I sighed. This was already shaping up to be an unpleasant conversation.

"No. I didn't notice anything strange last night. Why?"

I expected her to snap at me, or maybe criticize me for my dismissive attitude. It certainly wouldn't be the first time someone decided they didn't like me after a single meeting.

However, she just sighed and fell quiet for a moment, her exhaustion audible through the phone.

"Yesterday evening, when we were transporting the evidence we found on your property, some of it went... missing."

"Missing?" The last traces of sleep disappeared, and my mind suddenly felt sharp as a hunting knife. "What? You mean, like, someone stole the body?"

"No," she practically shouted in her rush to correct me. "No. The body is fine. But the objects we found in the coffin, the key and the journal, have disappeared, and we're not sure who stole them."

Climbing from my bed, I padded over to the window on bare feet, carefully stepping over Indigo, who was sleeping on the floor. Outside the window showed the view of the backyard. Everything looked the same as it had yesterday. A large hole in the ground surrounded by disturbed dirt and remains of broken concrete, and my carefully cultivated garden that now showed evidence of more footprints than I would like.

Even if someone was poking around the yard, I wouldn't be able to tell, everything was already so disturbed.

I held the phone up to my ear again.

"You think someone might be coming after me as well?"

Deputy Belrose sighed again. It seemed we were both doing a lot of that this morning.

"It's unusual for someone to go to such lengths to tamper with a case. Especially one so old, if our estimates about the body are correct. I doubt anyone will come after you since we've already got everything off your property, but we can't be too sure until we know exactly what's going on."

After again promising the Deputy that I hadn't noticed anything, and I would contact her if I did, I eventually managed to hang up the phone. Then, after staring out the window in a daze for a minute, I headed downstairs to start making coffee.

Since my own house wasn't finished yet, I was still living in Brody's place. This meant the house was set up to his liking and not my own. The kitchen was sparse but functional, with easy to clean metal countertops that contrasted with the warm wood constructing the rest of the house.

Every time I tried to do anything in his kitchen, I kept getting turned around. I swear the man had arranged everything in the exact opposite place from where I would have put it, but I wasn't about to dictate his organizational habits. It wasn't my house, after all.

The coffee machine, which was under the window in the exact place I would have chosen to put the kitchen sink, was one of the most modern things in the house. It could make two dozen different types of drinks, and I was certain Brody had tried them all. The man drank nearly as much caffeine as water.

In contrast, I went for a basic coffee with no extra bells or whistles.

As I was scooping the beans into the

machine, a thought struck me, and the bag slipped from my hand to spill all over the counter.

"Not everything."

Completely forgetting about coffee, I stared out the kitchen window at the spot on the porch where Deputy Belrose had revealed the objects found in the coffin.

A key, a journal, and a locket.

Except, only the key and the journal had been stolen because Trent requested to take the locket with him.

Whatever the mystery behind the body was, if the thief was willing to steal the first two objects, then they were going to want the third one as well.

Leaving the coffee where it had fallen, and silently apologizing to Brody for making a mess in his house, I ran back up to my room to throw on some clothes and grab my keys. There was probably less than ten minutes between the moments my phone woke me up and when I pulled my truck out of its parking spot, yet I felt like I still wasn't moving fast enough.

During our conversation yesterday, Trent had told me about the antique shop he owned, including the fact that he lived in an apartment above the shop. If I knew this after only a single conversation with him, then someone who was specifically targeting him would have no problem finding him.

The antique shop *Memory Lane* was technically within the heart of Emberwood, though not by much. The shop stood about one block from the official outskirts.

It was also, unfortunately, on the opposite side of town. Winding mountain roads made it impossible to get anywhere fast, so despite how quickly I left, it was another half hour before I pulled up in front of his shop.

As I drove, I tried to call Trent, but got

no answer. I reminded myself that it was early. The sun was barely up, and dusky blue reminders of the night sky still clung to the edges of sunrise. Emberwood's streetlights were still on, tricked by the shade of the surrounding forest into thinking the sun hadn't made an appearance yet. There was a very good possibility that Trent was simply asleep, and that was why he didn't pick up the phone. Yet, the longer I listened to the line ring, the more my anxiety grew.

I brought my truck to a stop right outside the antique shop, barely maintaining enough rational thought to avoid parking illegally. When I approached the door, I realized the shop was shut up tight. Metal panels covered the door and windows like a fortress preparing to defend against a siege. At first, this brought me a sense of relief that Trent had plenty of security measures in place. But then, the more I thought about it, the more worried I became.

These weren't standard security measures that a shop owner would set up before going to sleep. These were drastic measures someone would only activate in an emergency.

Now even more fearful than I had been a moment ago, I started banging on the door.

"Trent? You in there? It's me. Magnus. We met yesterday."

No response.

Not that I should have expected one when I was banging on the man's door like a madman.

Taking a deep breath, I forced myself to calm down and approach the situation more rationally.

A security system like this would have exterior cameras. If Trent was inside, he would no doubt be watching those cameras, so I could talk to him that way.

Searching the area above the door, I

found a camera right away, and positioned myself on the front step so I would be in full view facing the lens.

"Trent. I got a call from Deputy Belrose this morning. She said that the key and journal they found had gone missing. I'm worried that the thief might target you, too. I understand that you don't really have any reason to trust me but is there a way I can at least talk to you to make sure you're okay."

After a moment of silence, there was a click of an unlatching lock, and the reinforced door opened a crack.

"Are you alone?"

I couldn't see Trent through the inch gap that had been revealed, but I recognized his voice.

What I could see, however, was the unmistakable glint of a gun being pointed in my direction.

I raised my hands slowly to show I meant no harm and was unarmed. There was a knife hidden inside my boot, so it was technically a lie, but he didn't need to know that.

"Yeah. It's just me. Are you okay?"

The door closed, and my heart sank when I thought I'd somehow managed to scare him off. Then I heard more locks clicking, and the door re-opened all the way.

Trent stood off to the side of the doorway, waving me in.

"Hurry up and get in. I don't want to leave it open for long."

The moment I passed under the threshold, the door slammed behind me, and the complex locking system was set back into place.

Trent noticed me observing the door with curiosity, and his face bloomed crimson.

"My grandmother was paranoid about someone robbing the place, so she set up the security system. Didn't think I'd ever have to use it."

Then he remembered the gun in his hand, and his blush turned such a bright glowing red I could almost feel the heat radiating from his face a few feet away.

"Sorry about that." He stored the gun in a rack by the door. "It's been a... strange night."

I wasn't concerned about having a gun waved in my face. It certainly wasn't the first time, and even after retiring from the military, I doubted it would be the last. The only thing I was concerned about was the implication of his words.

"I take it something happened last night."

Trent let out a deep sigh—I could relate with the sentiment—and nodded.

"Come on. I just started making coffee. Let me get us something to drink and I'll tell you about it."

The little backroom of the shop was even more sparse than Brody's kitchen. A coffee machine was basically the only thing there. I hoped his apparent upstairs was better outfitted, but I wasn't about to ask. That was his personal business, and I was already intruding on his privacy just by being here.

With coffee mugs in hand, we found seats on a pair of couches too old and moth-eaten to sell but were still very comfortable.

Over the next twenty minutes Trent gave me a basic summary of what had happened last night, including his success at cleaning up the picture inside the locket, and his suspicions about the identity of the thief.

"Deputy Hillard? Really? Why? What's the point in stealing a hundred-year-old locket? He wasn't even alive when the person in the coffin was buried."

Trent set his mug aside, making sure to place it squarely on the crocheted coaster waiting on the end table to keep it off the wood.

"It's probably even older than that. After taking a better look at it, the locket is probably closer to a hundred and twenty-five or even a hundred and fifty years old."

I shrugged and also placed my empty mug on a coaster. "No matter how old it is, there's no reason to steal it. After you were done with it, you would have returned it to them. It would have been a lot easier to steal then, so why take the risk and jump the gun now?"

"I don't know." Trent toyed with his fingers as he spoke, never looking directly at me. "Assuming it actually is Deputy Hillard, maybe he didn't want to attract attention, or maybe he wanted to pin the theft on me. Who knows? It might not have even been the Deputy. It was dark last night. I might have seen it wrong. Shoelaces aren't exactly a reliable form of identification."

"What about the security cameras?" I asked, remembering the advanced security system still reinforcing the door. "Surely they recorded the attempted break in."

Trent nodded as he pulled a familiar locket out from his pocket. "They recorded the break in, but the cameras are mostly focused on the doors and windows, and they aren't good enough to pick up the exact color of someone's shoelaces at night." He let the long chain of the locket run through his fingers a few times, treating the antique with care even when he was absent-minded.

I grabbed his hands with my own, stilling the movement of his fingers so the cool metal of the locket was pressed between our palms.

"Let's assume for a second that what you saw was correct and it really was Deputy Hillard that tried to break in last night. Why? What's so special about this locket that he took the risk of breaking in rather than wait a few days for you to return it?"

Trent stared down at our clasped hands, and an attractive blush stained his cheeks. The man was cute, in a rugged way, and reminded me of Indigo and Onyx.

Strong on the outside, but a warm puppy on the inside.

He quickly shook off my hand when he seemed to realize how long he'd been staring, and instead, focused on opening the locket. The clasp was small and tricky, nearly slipping from his fingers a few times, but eventually, he managed to get it open and hand it to me.

"The only thing I can think of is the picture inside. Maybe Deputy Hillard didn't want me cleaning it up, but this image doesn't mean anything to me, so I don't know what the significance is."

Trent hadn't just been bragging when

he claimed he could restore the old picture. It still held the patina of age, but what had once been an indecipherable smudge was now a clear portrait of a woman."

She was a young woman, with perfectly styled ringlets in her hair, and dressed in what looked like old clothes but were probably the height of fashion at the time. The picture was black and white, so there was no telling what her coloring was, but something about her made me think she was blonde.

She was also not familiar at all. Not that I thought she would be, but Trent was right. There was nothing particularly earth-shattering about the picture that would explain why a member of law enforcement would try to break into a store in the middle of the night.

Still, something about it must be important, even if I couldn't see what it was. Just thinking about the possibilities, what would have happened if Trent didn't have such good security, made me shudder. Deputy Hillard was a member of law enforcement. That gave him a lot more resources than the average person.

During my service years, I'd seen plenty of higher-ups using their position to cover up crimes. Usually only small offences, but there had been a few major incidents that didn't bear repeating.

I'd hoped that I would be free from such abuse of power once I retired, but apparently that had been a foolish hope.

My thoughts were getting too depressing. Looking around the small backroom, which was stuffed with antiques, I searched for a change of topic.

"An antique store seems like a strange choice for you."

As soon as the words were out of my mouth, I wanted to smack myself. My affliction of "foot-in-mouth" disease was nothing new. It had gotten me into more than my fair share of trouble throughout my life, but just once I'd like to be able to hold a conversation without accidentally insulting the person I was talking to.

Luckily, Trent didn't take the comment personally. Rather than get offended, he threw his head back and laughed. It was a round, full-belled sound that filled the entire shop.

"I know. I don't look like the type to run an antique store. Most people get confused the first time they see me behind the counter. It was my grandmother's. I inherited it after..."

He trailed off, absently rubbing a hand over his knee. The silence lasted a moment before he gathered himself, like a general summoning his trips to battle, and continued.

"I used to do competitive weightlifting. There was an incident and... well, I ended up getting injured at a big competition. Tore the ligaments in both my knee and ankle, which put an end to my competition days. After that, I needed something to do, so I took over the shop from my grandmother, and now here I am."

At the end of his explanation, he held out his hands, showing off the shop around him. We were still sitting in the back room, so I couldn't actually see most of the shop, but what little I'd seen of it on the way was impressive, and the antiques around us were obviously well cared for.

"How long have you been running the place? It seems like you've put a lot of work into it, so you must love it."

"I do," Trent said as he picked up a music box that was sitting on a shelf next to him and turned the key. A soft melody started playing. "I was closer to my grandparents than my actual parents. They lived in the apartment above the shop, just like I do now, so I spent every minute I could over here. I think a lot of people forgot that I didn't actually live here. I would help with the shop, and my grandma taught me about the different antiques. It was nice."

The song ended, and Trent placed the music box back on its shelf, carefully aligning it into the exact spot it sat before.

"Come on. Let me show you around. Not to brag, but there's some pretty interesting stuff here." He stood up and was halfway out the door into the main part of the shop when he stopped and turned back to me. "If you want to, that is. I sometimes forget that not everyone finds this stuff as interesting as I do."

He'd looked so excited when he was talking about the shop, but the light in his eyes dimmed when faced with the reality that I might not care about something that was so important to him.

In that moment, I was prepared to write an essay on the importance of antiques, even though English was never my best subject in school. I jumped out of my seat, barely remembering the locket I still held.

"Nope. I'd love to see the shop. Show me what you got."

He could lecture me about the importance of every item in the shop if it kept that excited light glowing in his eyes.

The locket was placed into a small box on the front counter for safe keeping while Trent showed me some of the stuff the shop had accrued throughout the years. There were the usual things one would expect in an antique shop, such as old furniture, decorative lamps, and enough crockery to supply the entire town.

Yet there were also unexpected finds, such as rare musical instruments, expensive jade statues, and even a silk parasol.

My favorite were the collections, like a display box filled with rare coins laid out in neat rows, or a set of old Hot Wheel toys. There was something about the collection of it, and seeing all these objects that belonged together gathered in one place, that brought a sense of peace to my heart. On their own, these objects wouldn't be worth nearly as much, but together they increased each other's value exponentially.

One of the collections made me laugh out loud the moment I saw them.

"Playboy magazines? Really? Please tell me those were your grandmother's collection."

Trent laughed along with me as he spread some of the magazines over the table. "Partially. My grandmother still owned the shop when she got a few that were mixed in with a box of other magazines. She was going to throw them out, but I insisted that they could be valuable. Some of the really old ones are collector's items and can fetch a good price with the right buyer. At first, she thought I just wanted to keep them for myself, so that was when—"

His words came to such an abrupt stop that I had to look up at him to make sure he hadn't run face first into a brick wall. He was fine, yet he had a look on his face as though he'd been struck.

His eyes flickered my direction, but couldn't seem to focus on me, so he ended up staring at his hands as he shuffled the magazines around into an order that only made sense to him.

I placed a hand on his arm and couldn't help noticing the healthy amount of muscle that lay hidden under his sleeve. It shouldn't have been surprising for someone who used to compete in weightlifting, but still it was. Trent had the look of a large, but loveable teddy bear, so the hidden hardness under that exterior was a shock.

"You don't have to tell me if you don't want to."

Trent nervously cleared his throat a few times but didn't try to remove my hand. "No. I want to. I just haven't really talked about it before. My grandma thought I wanted the magazines for myself until... until I came out to her. Then she believed me."

An awkward air hung over him as he waited for my reaction while trying to pretend like what he just said wasn't important.

I'd been in his shoes before. Such conversations never got easier.

Flipping randomly through one of the magazines, I laughed quietly to myself. "You think that's bad? My family didn't believe me after I came out to them. For a year they thought it was a running joke I was putting on. Apparently, their only exposure to gay people were the stereotypes they saw in movies. To them I couldn't possibly be gay because I was too traditionally masculine."

The heavy weight that was hanging on Trent's shoulders slipped away so quickly it was like it never existed in the first place. Even his steps were lighter, practically bouncing on the balls of his feet, and he stepped a little closer to my side to lean against the table next to me.

"I suppose it can be hard to believe a kid when they come out with something like that, especially if they don't know much about LGBT stuff to begin with."

I snorted. It was an unattractive sound, but I couldn't help it. "I was in my thirties at the time."

Trent's voice was small as he just said, "Oh."

I could practically see the wheels turning in his head as he tried to figure out what to say next. Eventually, he just ended with "I'm sorry," and left it at that.

I tossed the magazine onto the table back with the others and picked up another one. This one was the oldest of the bunch, with the image of a woman in a swimsuit on the front. It was a one-piece suit that wasn't particularly risqué but was probably considered scandalous back in the nineteen fifties.

"Don't worry about it. They do believe me now. I think. Mostly, they just seem to ignore it and pretend I'm asexual. I suppose it doesn't really matter until I try to bring someone home. But, since I am perpetually single, that's not happening anytime soon, so it doesn't matter. I'll worry about it when the time comes."

"Would you?"

The question startled me, and I looked up from the magazine I'd been looking through just to have something to do with my hands.

"Would I what?"

"Introduce your partner to your family? You know, if you were dating someone?"

I shrugged. It wasn't a question I'd

thought about much before, as I had never gotten that far with anyone I had dated before.

Not that I had dated many people. Except for Brody and Creed, I'd kept my sexuality a secret in the military, so the relationships I had managed to maintain were short-lived.

Placing the Playboy back with the rest of its collection, I picked up another magazine from a different stack. This one turned out to be The Ladies' Home Journal and was even older than the Playboy had been. Back before photographs were even used, and everything within the publication was drawn by hand.

"If I was dating someone, then, yeah. I'd introduce them to my family. Eventually. I've hidden that part of myself for a long time due to my military career. But I don't have to do that anymore, so I'd like to start being more open."

We were close enough now that our arms were pressed against each other. I could feel the heat from his body even through both our clothes. The atmosphere around us was brittle, like we were standing on a frozen lake, uncertain about the thickness of the ice beneath us. There was a chance that we could walk to the other side without fear, but there was an equal chance that one step would send us plummeting into depths we couldn't recover from.

I wasn't sure which option I wanted to happen. Both were equally terrifying.

"I've only introduced one boyfriend to my family before. It was back when my grandparents were both alive. The whole thing was underwhelming. I don't know what I expected, but I guess I at least assumed there would be some reaction. Instead, my family acted exactly the same as if I'd just brought a friend over for dinner. I was newly eighteen at the time, so maybe they were just not used to thinking of me as an adult and having adult relationships, but I don't know. It never really sat right with me, but I couldn't complain either. They didn't technically do anything wrong."

The blush was back on his cheeks. It hadn't truly left from the moment I arrived, which was its own kind of compliment, but it flared up even brighter.

Somehow, I was actually managing to have a proper conversation with an attractive man without making a fool of myself. I was even—dare I say—flirting. It wasn't the most scandalous flirting, even the most puritanical grandmother wouldn't be sent clutching her pearls over our conversation, but it was more than I'd managed before.

It was certainly better than my disastrous attempts to talk with Carlton at the hardware store, if that could even be called a conversation.

I flipped through the pages of the magazine without even looking at it. The paper felt thin under my fingers, and lacked the glossy texture I was used to from magazines. One of the pages was loose, and I feared I would rip it if I handled it too roughly. As much as I didn't want to look away from Trent, I couldn't help looking down at the magazine in my hands to make sure I hadn't damaged part of his collection.

The image looking up at me from the magazine made me freeze.

"Hey, Trent, can I see that locket again?"

With a look of confusion, he snagged it from the little box on the counter and handed it over. "Sure, but why?"

"I might be wrong, but I think I found something."

Now that the locket had been opened a few times, the latch cooperated a little more easily. I laid the magazine open on the table and placed the equally open locket next to it.

One of the ads in the magazine selling perfume featured a picture of a woman sitting on an elaborate sofa, surrounded by other people like she was the life of the party. It was hand drawn, but incredibly realistic, and could almost be mistaken for a photo.

The picture in the locket showed the exact same woman.

Not just the same woman, but the exact same picture. It had been cropped to only show the woman's head and shoulders, but it was undeniably the same. Same face, same hairstyle, even the same outfit as the model in the magazine.

Trent and I stared at it for a moment, neither of us knowing what to say in response to our discovery.

"Sooooo," Trent mumbled, mostly to himself. "The picture from the locket was cut out of a copy of this magazine. Why?"

I checked the publisher's date on the magazine.

1901.

Based on Trent's estimated age for the locket, it was the right time, and not long before the fire that gave Emberwood its namesake.

The mystery of the locket and the body on my property might have nothing to do with the fire, but the fact that the two incidents happened so close together triggered my suspicion. I had no idea how the two incidents were related, or even what had happened to the body discovered on my property, but I felt certain that it was all tied together somehow.

Without warning, Trent suddenly snatched up the locket from the table and headed for the back of the shop

"Hey, Trent, wait," I called out as I followed him. "What are you doing?"

He didn't answer me as he searched through the drawers of a seemingly random desk.

"I know I had one," he said as he threw around the contents in the drawers. "It's got to be... ah ha."

Holding up his hand in victory, he held a small eye lens, like the kind jewelers used when studying small stones. It looked like an overly complicated monocle, especially when Trent hooked it over his ear, so it sat in front of one eye. Then he brought the locket up in front of his face while simultaneously adjusting the focus of the lenses on the jeweler's lens.

"What are you doing?" I asked again as I watched him.

Trent never stopped what he was doing, but he did answer me this time.

"We assumed that the picture was the reason why Deputy Hillard tried to steal the locket, but why would he need a cutout from a magazine? If the picture isn't important, then why go through the effort of hiding it in the coffin."

"You think there's something else that's special about the locket," I realized out loud.

He nodded while still turning the locket this way and that to observe it from every angle. "The picture might have even been a decoy to make it seem like a regular locket. If so, then that means we're overlooking something."

Even after turning it over several times, and testing every seam and joint on the locket, nothing seemed out of the ordinary. Randomly poking at the locket wasn't getting us anywhere, especially since we didn't even know what we were looking for. So, after about ten minutes of futile effort, I made a suggestion.

"Why don't we let my friend Brody take a look at it? He mostly works with wood, but he's done some metalwork as well, so he might have a better idea what to look for."

After a few minutes of debate, Trent eventually agreed. He locked the shop up so that it would remain safe even when he was gone and climbed into my truck with me.

As we drove away from the shop, the sun had barely risen above the horizon. The day had only just started, and I had a feeling it was only going to get more exciting.

We were halfway to my place, when I suddenly started laughing. Trent jumped and demanded to know what I was laughing about, but it took me a minute to calm down enough to explain.

Our earlier conversation had come true. I was bringing a man home, though it wasn't in the way I expected.

CHAPTER FOUR

Trent

I'D BEEN TO Magnus's place before, but it was different in the relaxed light of early morning without cop cars parked all over the lawn and a dozen people stomping over everything. The half-built clearing among the trees was peaceful, and I understood why Magnus wanted to retire here.

It was too bad that his retirement plans had been interrupted by a dead body.

Brody, the other owner of the property and Magnus's friend, was sitting on the front porch of the only finished house, drinking coffee from an oversized mug. Just as Magnus had described, he was a large ginger bear of a man that looked like a stereotypical lumberjack. He was already an intimidating sight, especially with two large dogs sitting at his feet—not to mention the small dog sitting in his lap and glaring at me like a judgmental old school master—but the sophisticated firearm hanging on the wall behind Brody's head said that there was more to the man than met the eye and he was not someone to mess with.

Swallowing heavily to hide my nerves, I approached the porch just a step behind Magnus.

As he watched us walking up, Brody didn't seem surprised by my arrival, but I could tell from the slight widening of his eyes that Magnus bringing someone to their property so early in the morning was not a common occurrence either.

"Mag," Brody greeted as the two of us approached the porch. "I heard you leave this morning, but I didn't realize you were bringing company back. Who's this?"

Although his words were technically polite, there was a frostiness to his tone that made me second-guess myself.

Had I misunderstood the relationship between the two men?

Magnus had said that he and Brody were friends from the military who decided to buy property together, but now that I thought about it, two men literally building a home together was more domestic than a standard friendship.

No, Magnus had said he was single. Surely, I couldn't have misunderstood such a straightforward statement. Besides, there was nothing going on between me and Magnus anyway. Perhaps I was just imagining Brody's tone, or it had nothing to do with me.

When he was on the porch, Magnus punched Brody in the arm, causing the rocking chair the other man was sitting in to sway backward.

"Shut up and finish your coffee, Brody. You're a bitch until you've had your caffeine. Trent, take a seat and show Brody what we found."

He pointed toward the third rocking chair on the porch. It was identical to the other two, and obviously placed there intentionally, which seemed like an odd choice. Only the two of them lived on the property.

What was the point of the third chair?

Pushing aside my questions about the chair, and the two men's overall arrangement, I took the locket out of my pocket to show it to Brody and explain what we'd found.

"So, you think there's something else unique about this locket," Brody concluded as he turned the locket over in his hands.

"There must be," Magnus said from where he was sitting in his own rocking chair, leaning so far forward that he was in danger of tipping over. "Why else would someone try to steal it? If the picture isn't important, then there must be some other secret about the locket. Plus, we can't go to the cops with this if they're the ones trying to steal it, so we came to you. I know you've done some metal work in the past and figured you might be able to see something about it that we missed."

Brody looked between the two of us for a moment, before grabbing Magnus by his braided hair and pulling him forward until he was bent sideways over the arm of his chair.

"What? Hey," Magnus flailed and grabbed his hair near the scalp to keep it from pulling too much. "Brody, man. Let go."

Brody only held on tighter.

"You're an idiot. Have you stopped to think that maybe he's lying to you? What proof does he have that anything he said actually happened? How do we know he's not involved somehow? Most people don't jump immediately to avoiding the police."

While what Brody said made logical sense, I couldn't help feeling insulted by his insinuation. Standing from my chair, I crossed my arms and looked down at him, for once using my full size to its advantage. If Brody stood up, we'd probably be about the same height, so my posturing lost some of its effect, but so long as he was sitting, I had the clear advantage.

"Avoiding the police makes sense when one of them tried to break into my shop. Believe me or not, I know what I saw. I can get you the video from my security cameras to prove it, but I'm sure you'll come up with a reason to distrust me anyway. Magnus came to me. I didn't ask for his help. If you don't want to get involved, that's fine. I'll take my property back and I'll leave so you don't have to hear from me again."

I reached for the locket, but Brody pulled it away.

"This isn't even your property. It was found on our property, which technically makes it ours, right? That means we decide what to do with it."

Before I could argue further, a snuffling sound caught my attention. The dogs lying at Brody's feet had stood up when I approached, and now the Rottweiler was sniffing my hand.

I held still, barely breathing as I waited to see what the dog would do. If I recalled correctly the dog's name was Onyx, but that wouldn't help me avoid canine judgment.

After a moment, Onyx licked my hand, then settled back down on the floor of the porch with a sigh like it had just put in a long hard day of work.

In response, Brody stood and clapped me on the shoulder. As I suspected, we were the same height, and despite all my years of strength straining, the force of his hand nearly made my knees buckle.

"Well, you've passed the initial inspection," Brody said, casting a fond glance down at the dogs near his feet. "Plus, I do like a man who stands his ground. All right. I'll trust you, for now. I can take a look at this locket, but no guaranties. I'm better with wood than metal."

Magnus also stood and shooed Brody's hand off my shoulder, grumbling under his breath the whole time.

"No reason to go through the whole suspicious act. Could have just trusted me from the beginning."

His complaining was cut off when Brody yanked on his braid again.

MAGNUS

"Your dick and your brain are mortal enemies that refuse to work at the same time. So, no, I don't trust you for shit right now. You get stupid around a handsome face and can get talked into anything."

Magnus grumbled some more and batted at Brody's hand until the other man let go. Brody went back inside the house, laughing all the while as he took the locket with him and left Magnus with a scowl and a messed-up braid.

"Bastard," Magnus continued to grumble as he untied his braid to comb his hair out straight. "I should shave myself bald just so he doesn't have anything to yank me around with anymore."

I had to turn away as Magnus ran his fingers through his hair. The first time I saw him at the cage match, his hair had been braided then, too, and I thought it looked nice then, but it was no comparison to the sight of it down. With his blond hair flowing down around his shoulders, he looked like the rugged hero I'd find on the cover of a bodice-ripper romance book. I would never admit it out loud, but my bookshelves were filled with several dozen books just like that, most of which I'd picked out based on the appearance of the male love interest on the cover.

Instead of Playboy magazines, my grandmother should have been keeping me away from her own bookshelves which was where I'd picked up my first romance novel, the covers of which had been my personal fantasy material for years until I discovered the true wonders of the Internet. Now that I had a man just like the subject of my fantasies standing in front of me, I didn't know what to do with myself. I was no heroine, and this was no romance book. Nothing I had ever read prepared me for this interaction.

"Sorry about him," Magnus said once he finished tying his hair up again. This time, he'd forgone the braid and decided to just tie his hair into a simple low ponytail. "Brody isn't usually so suspicious, but this is a strange situation. Plus, he's right. I do tend to go stupid around attractive men."

I managed to drag my gaze away from his ponytail, which was almost as distracting as seeing his hair free, to catch the last part of his statement.

"Does that mean you find me attractive?"

Along with his blond hair, Magnus's skin was also very fair, so the bright red blush that overcame his face was even more noticeable.

Clearing his throat, Magnus started walking away. "It'll take some time for Brody to look over the locket, so I'm gonna take care of some other stuff while we wait. Feel free to just sit here and relax in the meantime."

His words almost sounded casual, but he tripped when he accidentally missed the last step off the porch.

I laughed to myself and followed him. Magnus was a confident force of nature when he was fighting, but outside the ring he was just a big dork.

"I'd rather stay busy than just sit around. What were you planning to do? Maybe I can help."

When Magnus looked back at me over his shoulder, most of the blush had left his face, but there was still a tint of pink on his cheeks.

"Those cops made a mess of my garden when they were here yesterday, so I need to get it sorted out if I want to have any hope of a harvest this year. I could use another set of hands with that."

"I have hands," I said with a cheeky smile on my face. "Just tell me what to do with them."

MAGNUS

Just as I'd hoped, Magnus blushed again and started walking faster.

The confirmation that he did in fact find me attractive gave me a surge of confidence that I hadn't felt in years. Suddenly, I couldn't help but want to tease him, and the flirty conversation between us came much more naturally.

My first time on the property, I'd noticed the half-finished house but hadn't really thought about it too much. Apparently, the plan was for each of them to have their own house, along with a third house for another friend who was going to join them later once he finished his military service. Brody's house had been completed quickly, but Magnus's was taking much longer since he was more focused on the land.

I'd also gotten a glimpse of the garden behind Magnus's half-finished house when I was there the first time, but I hadn't realized how extensive it was.

When he talked about a harvest, he wasn't kidding. There was enough tilled soil and various kinds of crops to almost be considered a small farm, especially with the abundant chicken coop.

It would have been an impressive sight, if not for the fact that a fourth of the garden had been trampled under the feet of so many cops coming and going yesterday. Looking at the stalks of broken plants and unearthed roots, I nearly wept at the thought of so much wasted work.

Magnus just sighed and handed me a shovel.

"There's no use getting mad about it," he said as he dug his own shovel into the dirt. "No amount of anger will bring the plants back to life."

He directed me toward which rows needed to be dug up, saying I didn't need to be careful so long as I stayed within the area he indicated. All of it needed to go.

Most of the plants were still young and

the sprouts all looked the same to me. I dumped broken stalks and balls of dirt into the nearby wheelbarrow indiscriminately, without any idea of what I was handling. Yet, Magnus was able to identify every plant with barely a glance. He could tell a strawberry plant from a pepper plant just from the shape of the leaves, and even tried to explain the difference to me.

It all went right over my head.

After about an hour of digging, we had about half the damaged area cleared out. We stopped to take a break, and Magnus fetched us some water. Even up in the mountains the midsummer sun was unforgiving, and I was reminded why I preferred to workout out at an indoor gym rather than playing outdoor sports.

"You know, this is pretty impressive," I said as I leaned against my shovel. "How'd you learn all this stuff? I tried helping my grandma with her garden once when I was a kid, and ended up picking half her flowers because I couldn't tell them apart from the weeds."

Magnus shrugged as he took a long drink, and I watched a drop of water escape his lips and slide down his neck.

I could so easily lean over and lick that drop of water away. There was barely a foot of space separating us. I didn't actually do it since we weren't that familiar with each other yet, but the thought was there at the forefront of my mind.

Magnus caught my gaze and must have been able to read my thoughts in my eyes, because he immediately choked and started coughing.

I patted him on the back until he could breathe again.

Even once he stopped coughing, his voice still sounded a bit raw.

"It's, um... you know, it's funny. People always think there must be some reason behind my love for plants. Like the only reason I'd like gardening was if it was connected my mother, or something." He took another drink, slowly this time, and wiped his mouth with the back of his hand before another drop could escape.

I withheld my disappointment.

"I'm not criticizing anyone who does like something because of the connection to their family," he quickly clarified. "The fact that you like antiques because of your grandmother is great. I'm just saying, there isn't any story behind it for me. I've just always had a thing for plants. I like how they can always start over. Even if a plant dies, once you clear out the old roots and plant new ones, it'll grow again. Just like what we're doing here. Part of the garden was destroyed but give it time and soon you won't be able to tell which plants are new and which ones are old."

After another hour of work, we

managed to get the rest of the destroyed plants dug up and were left with a patch of bare dirt. I thought that would be it, but then Magnus brought out bags of more dirt, which were apparently different than the regular dirt.

"The ground here isn't fertile enough on its own," Magnus explained as we spread the new dirt over the old dirt. "I haven't had time to get a composting station started to make my own soil mixture, so I've bought the pre-fertilized stuff for now. This will help the plants grow better than if we just planted them straight into the bare ground."

The whole process of re-*dirt*ifying the dirt took longer than expected, and it was well past noon by the time we were staring at the freshly arranged dirt patch.

"There's a lot more steps to this than I thought there was," I said as I wiped the sweat from my brow.

Magnus handed me another glass of

water. "Gardening isn't easy. I don't know why people always make fun of it as a thing that only little old ladies do when there's so much work involved. Right now, this garden is still small enough to manage by hand, but eventually, when I expand it, I'll probably have to get some machines to help me out."

I eagerly accepted the water, and drank most of it in one go, barely coming up for air.

"Are you really planning on building a greenhouse on top of all this? The garden you have now already seems like enough."

At the edge of the garden, I watched a line of fruit trees swaying in the breeze. I couldn't tell what kind they were, as all trees looked the same to me, but I was certain that they would soon be heavy with the literal fruits of Magnus's labor.

Magnus sighed as he looked at the torn up concrete area where his dreams of a greenhouse had been disrupted.

"Strictly speaking, I don't *need* a greenhouse. We could get by with just the garden, but then we're limited to only eating seasonal local produce. A green house would let me grow things year-round, and I won't be limited to plants that are naturally suited to the area." He grinned at me, and in that moment, I could easily picture him as the young boy he used to be. "Strictly speaking, I'd love some fresh pineapple, but it's not going to grow up in the mountains without a lot of help."

With delighted barking, the pit bull came bounding over to us. The dog's paws never touched the freshly laid soil, and it sat on the edge of the garden, repeatedly calling for our attention.

"Yeah, yeah, Indigo," Magnus replied to the dog. "We're coming." He then took the shovel out of my hands. "Come on. Brody must have something for us."

Brody stood in the doorway to his

house, barring us from entry when we stepped up on the porch.

"Oh, no. Magnus, you know the rules. You're not tracking all that dirt in the house. Wash off with the hose and leave your shoes outside."

Magnus rolled his eyes but complied and led me over to the hose connected to the side of the house. "I swear, he sounds more and more like my mother every day."

Apparently, we weren't out of hearing range, because Brody shouted at us from the doorway.

"I'll beat your ass like your mom did, too, if you set one dirty boot inside my house. I built this place with my own hands, and I'm keeping it clean. When your own house is finished, you can tack mud wherever you want."

Using the hose, we washed off our hands and faces, and left our shoes on the porch just like Brody wanted. Waiting on the table inside the house was a pile of cold sandwiches, and my stomach growled at the sight. I hadn't realized how hungry I was until that moment, especially after skipping lunch, and immediately grabbed a sandwich once given permission.

Magnus may have been joking when comparing Brody to a mom, but between the insistence on cleanliness and making us lunch, that's exactly what it felt like.

Since Brody forbade us from taking food out of the kitchen for fear of getting crumbs everywhere, he brought the locket out to us in order to show off what he'd found while we finished eating.

"See this seam here?" He used a long thin needle to point at one of the welded seams hidden right under the decorative rose on top of the locket. Even with a magnifying glass it was hard to see, and with the naked eye it was nearly impossible. "It doesn't stand out at first, but the natural striations in the metal line up on either side of the weld."

Magnus and I bore similarly confused looks, and after sighing for a moment, Brody explained further. "To put it simply, the rose and the top panel of the locket were cast together as one piece. There'd be no reason to weld them together, unless the rose was cut off after the locket was already made and then reattached."

Although he didn't say it outright, the implication was obvious. Someone had hidden something inside the locket. It was a rather large locket, and although the rose was fairly flat, there was still enough space for a decently sized pocket in the metal.

Assuming whatever the person wasn't to hide wasn't too large. It couldn't be much bigger than a quarter, but after years running an antique shop, I'd learned that the size of an object didn't always correlate to its value.

Sometimes the smallest things were

worth the most.

"So, how do we open it?"

Brody and Magnus kept scowling at the locket.

"Should we open it?" Brody asked. Magnus immediately opened his mouth to argue, but Brody cut him off. "No, wait, hear me out. I've been thinking about this, and I've been wondering if we should get involved at all. Someone's already tried to break into Trent's place, so obviously there's something going on, but it doesn't actually concern us."

I pushed around the crust of my sandwich on my plate, silently torn between two different feelings. On the one hand, I was glad Brody now believed me about the break in and seemed to trust me, but on the other hand, I hated that what he was saying made sense.

Magnus must have also been having similar conflicted feelings because his voice wavered when he spoke up.

MAGNUS

"We can't just... not open it. Can we?"

"I mean, we could," Brody shrugged. "This isn't our problem. Our connection to any of this is that the coffin happened to be found on our property. We could hand the locket back to the police and wash our hands of the whole situation. Right now, our involvement has been minimal, but if we choose to open this locket, then we can be accused of tampering with police evidence. So, before we go messing with this locket anymore, we have to make a choice. Do we get involved or not?"

An old clock ticked away somewhere in the living room as the three of us stared at the locket in silence.

"We have to open it," Magnus eventually said.

He reached for the locket, but Brody slapped his hand away. "Now, hold on. There are three of us involved. You can't just make that decision on your own.

Trent, what about you? The police left the locket with you, and you're the one whose home was almost broken into. What do you think we should do?"

I wanted to agree with Magnus and say that we should open it, but one thought held me back.

"I think... you should make the final call Brody. You're the only one who knows how to work with metal. You'll be the one who has to physically open it, and if we end up pissing off the wrong people, they could come after you for it, so this should be your call."

Leaning both of his hands against the kitchen counter, Brody stared down at the locket, glaring at it like he was trying to intimidate the metal into revealing its answers.

"Ugh." He growled and ran two exasperated hands through his hair. "I want to say we should just walk away, but damn it all, I saw too many corrupt officers getting away with shit during my service time. I hate the idea of some corrupt cop running around in my new home. All right. We'll open it but give me some time to see if there's a way to open it without destroying the locket. If we're lucky, maybe no one has to know that we opened it at all."

Magnus and I eventually left Brody to investigate the locket further, and we returned to the garden to continue our work as well. With the fresh soil laid down, we still had to plow it into proper rows before we were ready to plant anything, plus the rest of the garden that was still thriving couldn't be ignored. By the end of the day, we still hadn't planted anything, but the garden was ready to go and as soon as the sun rose the next day, then we could start seeding the ground.

I'd never been the kind of person to do manual labor outside of the gym but looking over the garden that we'd put so much into, I found it more rewarding than I expected.

As Magnus and I were herding the chickens into their coop for the night, Brody came running out of the house to shout at us from the porch.

"I think I got it."

We finished up with the chickens and cleaned up as quickly as we could, then joined Brody inside the house. Once again, we huddled around the kitchen table, but this time, with the light from the setting sun pouring in the through the window and staining everything red, we were surrounded by a very different atmosphere.

Brody used the same needle as earlier to point at one particular petal on the locket's rose. "I kept the idea of the natural striations of the metal in mind and looked for any other disturbances to the design. This petal is made from the same metal, but it has a different pattern to it, meaning it was cast on its own. So, I kept tinkering around with it, and I discovered this."

Picking the locket up oddly in his hand, he pressed down on the locket's regular latch as if he was going to open it the usual way, then pulled up on that singular petal at the same time. He needed Magnus's help to do both at once, meaning it wasn't something that could be done by accident, and we all watched as the rose petal pulled out from the rest of the flower.

Something clicked inside the locket.

"That's as far as I got," Brody said as he held the locket in both hands. "I didn't want to open it without you here."

Magnus and I both nodded, telling him to go ahead.

When Brody pulled on the rose, it completely detached from the rest of the locket, revealing a hidden hollow inside. A single piece of folded paper fell out from the hollow, barely bigger than a quarter.

It was old and yellowed with age. I couldn't tell without further testing, but the paper was probably as old as the locket itself.

With careful fingers, Brody unfolded the paper, which was wrapped around several small brown objects.

They rattled like stones when he dumped them onto the counter.

At first my brain didn't register what I was seeing, until Magnus spoke up next to me.

"Are those... coffee beans?"

CHAPTER FIVE

Magnus

WE ALL STARED at the beans on the counter for a moment, until Brody looked up at me.

"What're you asking me for? You're the plant guy, Mag. You tell me."

I picked one of them up, holding it under the magnifying glass Brody had used to show us the thin seams in the metal of the locket.

They were definitely coffee beans. I couldn't recognize the exact type just by looking, but there was nothing noteworthy about them that seemed worth stealing. Yet, someone had gone through the effort of hiding them in a coffin.

Remembering what else the coffin held, it seemed like these beans may have even been worth killing for.

"Hey, wait," Trent suddenly spoke up, pulling my attention away from the coffee beans. "What's this?"

He flipped over the paper that the beans had been wrapped in to reveal a drawing on the other side. At first it looked like just a collection of random lines, shapes, and other meaningless symbols. Completely incomprehensible to my eye, but Brody made a sound of recognition.

"It's a map," he said as he traced a finger over some of the lines.

I looked at the map again, trying to see what he saw.

"That's not like any map I've ever seen. It looks like a child's scribbles."

"No, see, look here." He pointed at a cluster of rectangles near the corner of the page. "That's the old mill out on the edge of town. And this is the creek that runs right next to it."

The squiggly line next to the rectangles did bear some resemblance to the river. I'd never looked at the whole river from a top-down perspective, but the double loop that resembled a pair of bunny ears was familiar. There was a good spot right between the two loops for fishing, where the water was deep and calm.

"All right, let's say this is a map of the area. What's it for?"

Brody grinned as he pointed to a spot on the complete opposite side of the paper. "What's any map for? X marks the spot."

Under his finger, an X had been drawn with such force that it indented the paper.

It also looked like it might have been drawn with a different colored ink, but time had faded it to the same sepia brown as everything else.

Based on the size of the river, I tried to judge the distance in my mind. Our property was on the north side of town, but the spot on the map seemed to be somewhere off to the east and was way out in the middle of the forest.

"That's further than I could hike in a day, especially cutting through untamed land. It'd be a two-day trip, at least. Maybe more depending on the terrain. Draw me up a better map, one that includes topography, and I'll plan something out."

"Hold on. Hold on," Trent interrupted, holding out both his hands like he meant to physically restrain Brody and me. "Are you actually planning on going out there? We have no idea what this map leads to, if it even leads to anything. It could be dangerous."

Brody and I shared a look, then both shrugged at the same time. Although we didn't say anything, I knew we were both thinking the same thing.

We'd already agreed to go through with it the moment we opened the hidden compartment in the locket. Now all we could do was see the mission through until the end.

"We've done stuff like this before," I tried to reassure Trent. "It's not really that different from a lot of the military missions we've been on."

Brody pulled out his phone and was already looking up more recent topographical maps of the area. "Besides, we won't be able to figure out how to handle this until we know what we're dealing with. Whoever tried to break into your place knows you have the locket, and probably already knows you're here with us. It won't be long before they also realize we've figured out what the locket was hiding, so we need to press our advantage while we can."

Trent crossed his arms and grumbled under his breath, "I know who tried to break in. I just don't know why."

Brody tapped the map again, right over the X. "And finding out where this map leads could tell us why. It's the only lead we've got."

The smirk that came to Brody's face was one of his few mean expressions. The man was usually very amenable, but when he got bitchy, it was always in a subtle way that left the other person unsure if they'd been insulted or not.

"Unless you know something about those coffee beans that you're not telling us. In that case, we'd be happy to let you take the lead here."

Before he'd even finished speaking, I punched Brody in the arm. "Don't be an ass. It was his shop that was attacked.

He's got reasons to be worried."

Brody rubbed his arm, but the cruel smirk dropped from his face. "And the body was found on our property. We've got reasons to be worried, too. I don't like not knowing who we're dealing with or why this is so important. Following the map will at least give us some answers."

"Fine," Trent agreed, and I was glad to see he didn't look too put out by Brody's comment. "But I'm coming, too."

My first thought was to immediately deny him, but I held my tongue. If I was in his shoes, I'd want to be involved as well.

As if predicting my argument, Trent rushed to keep talking.

"I've been camping before. It may not be the same as a military mission, but I won't be completely useless. I can carry my own weight."

I couldn't help letting my gaze flicker down his body, taking note of the strong physique hidden under his soft outer layer of comfort.

"I'm sure you can."

"All right," Brody interjected, raising an eyebrow at me and silently saying he knew exactly what direction my thoughts had gone. "You two will head out tomorrow. It'll be suspicious if we all disappear, so I'll stay here to try and make it look like we haven't gone anywhere."

The sun was already set, and the hour was starting to get late. With a plan of action decided, we heated up some leftovers that Brody had in his fridge for dinner. While we were eating there was a brief discussion about taking Trent back home that was immediately thrown out. His shop had already been targeted once. Even with his advanced security system, I didn't feel comfortable leaving him alone.

Plus, I wasn't going to complain about having him spend the night.

MAGNUS

Brody's house only had two bedrooms. The master bedroom was his, and I slept in the guestroom until my house was finished. This meant there weren't many places for Trent to sleep. The couch was an option. Brody and I were both large men, and we'd picked out furniture to fit us, so the couch would have enough room for him to sleep.

However, we were going to be roughing it in a tent for a few days, and he needed to get as much sleep as possible beforehand. I had a disassembled bed stored away, which I was planning to put in my own house once it was finished, so I offered to assemble the bed in Brody's guestroom. There wouldn't be much space left in the room with two beds, but it would be comfortable enough for one night.

By the time the bed was assembled, it was time to sleep, and we quickly called it a night.

The two of us were of a similar enough size that my clothes would fit him, so I left him a pair of pajamas. It was only when I was standing in the small space between the beds, clothing in hand, that I realized the problem I'd made for myself.

"Um, I'll, uh..." I could feel my cheeks starting to heat up, and practically threw the clothing against his chest. "I'll go change in the bathroom."

I fled before he could respond, but I swear I could hear him laughing at me.

By the time I came back from the bathroom, he'd already changed and was sitting on one of the two beds. My clothing fit him well enough, but there were areas where we differed, and nowhere was this more obvious than his legs. Trent must have never skipped leg-day even once in his life, because the shorts I'd given him were stretched taught across his thighs and the muscle of his calves was so pronounced it practically made a right angle.

Swallowing heavily, I tried not to let my gaze linger too long as I made my way over to the other bed.

"Sorry to make you share your bedroom," he said as I tossed my dirty clothes into the waiting hamper.

I still couldn't face him directly and gave more focus than necessary to rearranging the pillows on my own bed. "It's fine. It's not even my bedroom. It's Brody's guestroom. Besides, we're going to be sleeping in much closer quarters on the trip since we've only got one tent."

I froze and the pillow I was holding dropped onto the bed with a surprisingly loud sound.

Oh shit.

I hadn't even thought about it until that moment, but there was no way to make such a long hike in a single day. The two of us were going to be sharing a single tent. It was technically built for two people, but since we were both bigger than average, there wasn't going to be any space between us.

Even just imagining it, I could already feel myself growing hard inside my shorts. I bit the inside of my cheek to keep from reacting.

Human bodies were so stupid. I should be able to control my reactions better, but here I was, pitching a figurative tent just from the thought of pitching a literal tent. I hadn't been so easily reactive since I was a teenager, and even then, I'd never had to deal with it while the object of my attraction was in the room with me.

"I'm sure it'll be fine," Trent was saying, but I barely heard him, too caught up in my own mini crisis.

I somehow managed to go through the motions of turning off the lights and getting myself into bed without revealing my embarrassing state, but I couldn't fall asleep. Even with the familiar sounds of the forest just outside my window, which I usually found soothing, I laid awake watching the moonlight slowly move across the wall.

My arousal had calmed down, but I could still feel it simmering under my skin just waiting to rise again every time I heard Trent breathe just a few feet away. This trip was going to be a nightmare.

A pleasant yet torturous nightmare.

Closing my eyes, I eventually managed to convince myself to sleep by counting my breaths, both eager for and dreading the morning that was swiftly approaching.

***

When Brody and I first moved to our new property, there had been almost nothing here. The few structures that still stood were so weathered with time that they were little more than stacks of firewood. So, the two of us had been forced to literally camp out on the land until we managed to procure a couple of old RVs to act as shelter while we got Brody's house built.

Because of this, we still had plenty of camping gear lying around, and wouldn't have to waste time buying anything new. We woke up extra early to get the camping gear packed and review our route to make sure we knew exactly where we were going. It would take at least one night and two days to go there and back, assuming we turned around immediately after locating whatever the map led to. If we spent any time at the location, we'd probably have to spend a second night camping.

So, just to be sure, we packed enough supplies for two nights and three days. I would carry the tent while Trent carried the bulk of our food and water, so we each ended up shouldering the same load.

After some debate, we decided to head off directly from the house, rather than having Brody drive us to a closer starting point. There was a high probability that someone was watching us, and it would look suspicious if all three of us drove somewhere and only Brody returned. Plus, the location we were headed to was in the middle of nowhere. None of the town's roads went anywhere near it, so starting from the house wouldn't add that much to our journey.

The sun had only been up for about an hour when Trent and I headed off with camping gear strapped to our backs and a map that Brody had programmed into a satellite GPS leading our way.

The shade of the woods was pleasantly cool around us, just enough to cut down the heat of summer. Birds sang all around us, checking in with each other and celebrating another night they had survived as nocturnal predators settled down to sleep.

I'd hiked through several mountains

over the years, and although I had never traveled through the Rocky Mountains before, I had a better idea of what to look for. For the first hour of our journey, I was mainly focused on instructing Trent. I pointed out pitfalls in the ground he needed to look out for, and tricks for navigating such untamed land. He'd done plenty of hiking before, but always on a beaten path, so there were things he didn't know. Such as how to conserve energy by always picking the most even places to put his feet and not stepping up or down if he didn't have to, and how to spot hidden tripping hazards.

This kind of hiking was much harder and slower than he was used to, but the man's powerful legs came in handy, and he managed to keep up without exhausting himself.

After the first hour, we fell into an easy rhythm, and our conversation turned more casual. He asked how I'd learned so much and about my time in the military, so I told him a few anecdotes, including how I'd initially met Brody and Creed.

It had been my first real assignment out of boot camp. Brody, as the oldest of us, had a little more experience, so he had some idea what to expect, but Creed and I had been completely wet behind the ears. Back then, we were just kids playing pretend at being soldiers. We'd been sent on what should have been a relatively easy mission. All we had to do was guard a supply shipment of new weapons that were being transported to a different base. The territory we were cutting through was supposed to be safe and we were only meant to be extra back up. Then, halfway to our destination, the supply caravan had been bombed. I was knocked out, and when I woke up, I was bound in the back of a truck with Creed and Brody lying next to me.

As I got to this part of the story, Trent

stared at me with wide eyes. We'd stopped to rest, and he was taking a drink from his canteen, but he froze with it halfway to his mouth. A few drops of water trailed from the corner of his mouth, mixing with the sweat already running down his neck, but he didn't notice.

"Wait. You were captured?"

I took a long swig of my own water, swishing it around my mouth to chase away the taste of my own sweat, before continuing the story. "Yep. Three little baby soldiers, about to become POWs on their first mission."

I could laugh about it now, and when I recited the story, I always told it with confidence. What I would never tell anyone was that at the time I'd been pants-shittingly scared. All three of us had been. If I'd been alone, I probably would have just given up.

"So, what happened?" Trent asked as he put his water away, sitting on a rock like a child settling down for story time.

I shrugged, trying to act casual, and like I wasn't summarizing one of the most terrifying moments of my life.

"Well, we did the only thing we could do. We fought. We all knew that if our captors managed to take us to wherever we were headed, then we'd be done for. Our only hope was to escape while still in transit. So, that's exactly what we did."

This was usually the part of the story where most people looked impressed, but the expression on Trent's face was one of concern as he eyed me up and down.

"But how did you escape? I can't imagine your captors allowed you to keep your weapons."

"Didn't need 'em." I held up my fists, showing off the numerous scars lining my knuckles. "I've always been best at fighting hand-to-hand. So, we pulled a classic fake-out." Then I lifted my shirt so he could see the thin line of scar tissue cutting across my ribs. "I'd been grazed by a bullet in the initial attack. Nothing too bad, but it bled like hell. So, I played it up and made it seem like I was really injured. When one of our captors came to check on us, I jumped the bastard and slammed my bound hands into his face so hard I knocked him out in one hit. Then we took his weapons, cut off our bonds, and shot our way to freedom."

Trent reached toward me, and for a moment I thought he meant to touch my scar. I braced myself for the feeling of skin-to-skin contact, but instead, he pulled up my shirt a little higher to reveal the tattoo just above the scar.

I couldn't see if from my point of view, but I remembered every detail. It was a POW symbol but broken like a shattered mirror. Under the broken symbol were the words *Not Today.*

"Oh, yeah. That." I lifted my arm more so he could see the full thing. "Brody,

Creed, and I all got matching ones. There was talk about awarding us Prisoner of War status, but since our capture wasn't fully complete and we managed to escape before we were properly imprisoned, the higherup's decided not to award us. So, we tattooed ourselves with our own badge of honor over the injuries we sustained. Creed broke his wrist and had to have it surgically re-set, so the tattoo covers the surgery scar, and Brody was stabbed in the leg so it's on his calf.

The unexpected heat of Trent's hand on my skin made me jump. He traced his fingers over the tattoo, then trailed down to the scar to feel the raised edges there. The gentle feathering of his fingers over my skin made goosebumps rise and an electric sizzle shot to my groin.

"They should have awarded you with something. You were lucky to survive."

"What? Nah." I shoved my shirt back down, which conveniently also blocked his access to my skin. "I understand why they didn't give us anything. It wasn't actually that bad. Creed's real good at all the wilderness survival stuff, so we managed to find our way back to base without much issue."

I stood and hoisted my bag onto my back, making an exaggerated groan under the weight.

"I wish Creed was here right now. This hike would be a breeze for him."

Three more months, I reminded myself. Only three months until Creed's last deployment ended, and then the three of us would be back together again like we should be. Maybe then life would stop feeling so off balance.

I looked over at Trent as he settled his own bag on his back, barely even seeming to notice the weight on his shoulders.

No, even once Creed returned, I would still feel off balance so long as Trent was around. Handsome men like him always made me feel mixed up inside, like I didn't know which way was up anymore.

Add to that the fact that Trent was also nice, got along with my dogs, and didn't mind listening to me ramble on about plants for hours, I could so easily see myself falling in love.

It wouldn't be the first time. Creed and Brody said I fell in love too easily, and they were right. There had been several times before where I'd met a man, fallen head-over-heels right away, and built up this whole picture in my mind of the relationship we would have. Then I'd either find out that he was straight, or in the case where the object of my obsession was also gay, that they were just using me for sex.

Apparently, I didn't look like the type of guy to "settle down." Between my military history, my side-job as a cage fighter, and my overall roguish appearance, they always assumed I was some kind of wild soul. Someone who was down for a good time, but who would then leave in the morning.

I'd almost gotten used to the disappointed looks I would receive when it turned out that not only was I still there in the morning, but I was also trying to make them breakfast.

My thoughts were turning maudlin as I remembered my failed attempts at romance in the past, so I turned to something that always cheered me up.

Plants.

I started pointing out different noteworthy plants we passed on our hike and filled the air between us by telling Trent everything I could remember about them. The topics ranged from how to tell true morels and false morels apart, to the etymology behind the Orchid's name, to which pine needles were best for brewing into tea.

Trent listened to it all with rapt

attention, asking questions when necessary and adding in his own tidbits of info wherever he could. Before I knew it, miles had passed under our feet and the sun was starting its return journey back toward the horizon.

Under such foliage, we couldn't see the sky clearly, and cellphone coverage was spotty so far up in the mountains, but the clock on our GPS said it was approaching six o'clock in the evening. We only had a few hours of daylight left, so we started looking for a good place to set up camp. It took us about an hour to find a spot flat enough for the tent, and far enough away from any natural hazards.

From there, it was a simple matter of dividing up the tasks. Since I'd carried the tent, Trent volunteered to set it up while I got a fire started to boil some water for dinner. It was nearly dark by the time we finished, and the sweat left on my skin from the heat of the day chilled under the evening air. I shivered, but as much as I wanted a proper bath, that wasn't possible out in the wilderness. While waiting for the water to boil, I snuck down to the nearby stream. After splashing the cold water onto my face, I dipped a cloth into the stream and used it to wipe down my neck and torso. It wasn't as good as a bath, but it would have to do, and the cold water on my skin did leave me feeling somewhat refreshed.

"Good idea," Trent said as he knelt beside me. "I've sweat so much I think my shirt could stand up on its own right now."

He pulled the offending shirt right off over his head, tossing it aside, and giving me a clear view of his naked chest.

His shoulders were just as well built as I expected, but his time sitting behind a desk in his shop had left a healthy layer of softness over his chest and stomach. I knew if I grabbed him, he would be a fascinating combination of soft and hard. I nearly gave into the urge when he ran the wet washcloth over his chest, leaving behind water droplets caught in the hair there.

It would be so easy to just reach out for him, but I bit the inside of my cheek and held myself back.

Then I noticed how his nipples had hardened under the cool night air, and nearly died.

"I think the water should be done," I said as I quickly stood up, turning away from Trent so he wouldn't notice the erection blooming under my pants. "Just give me a minute to get the food ready."

I hurried back to the fire pit, and after retrieving a new shirt for myself, I pulled the boiling pot off the flames. The hot water was then added to two packets of dehydrated food, which I sealed and set aside as I waited for our meals to set up.

After another minute, Trent sat on a

log across from me. He was still shirtless, but he was searching through his bag for more clothes, so I kept my eyes averted until he was covered again.

"I'd say that smells good," Trent said as he finally pulled on a new shirt. "But I'm so hungry that anything would probably smell good right now, so I can't really compliment your cooking."

I poked at the fire with a stick, rearranging the burning logs as if they needed my help to do their job. "Don't bother. These dehydrated meals aren't really meant to taste that great. They're just meant to be efficient. But, hey, they're at least better than MREs. So that's something. Good job with the tent, by the way. You got that up really fast."

I hadn't even looked at the tent, and quickly snuck a look over my shoulder to make sure the tent was, in fact, standing.

It was, and from what I could tell, it was properly anchored to the ground as well.

"Thanks," Trent said as he stretched out his legs, crossing one ankle over the other like the log he sat on was a luxury armchair in disguise. "I am good at erecting things, if nothing else."

He looked right at me as he said it, not even trying to hide his double entendre.

I cursed under my breath and accidentally jabbed the fire so hard one of the logs rolled away from the fire pit. My reaction to him had not gone unnoticed as I had hoped. He probably noticed my reaction last night as well, and I'd only been fooling myself all this time.

With the toe of his boot, Trent nudged the burning log back into place.

"You know I don't mind, right?"

"What?" I looked up at him with wide eyes, trying my best to play dumb.

He just raised an eyebrow at me, the firelight making his features even more pronounced. "I don't mind that you're turned on by me. In fact…"

He leaned closer, stretching his hand across me until he completely blocked the firelight, and I was consumed by the darkness of his shadow.

"…that's what I'm hoping for."

As I was left speechless, he snagged one of the meal pouches from my other side and sat back in his previous spot by the fire.

"I think they're done now," he grinned at me, then set about eating like he hadn't just stolen all the air from my lungs with a single sentence.

"Yeah," I said, not even sure what I was agreeing to as I blindly reached for the remaining meal pouch.

I ate mechanically, barely noticing what I put in my mouth. A heat boiled under my skin that had nothing to do with the outer temperature.

I'd finished most of my meal, not tasting a single bit of it, when I heard

MAGNUS

Trent sigh. At first, I didn't look up, until the sudden feeling of his hand on my arm made me jump.

"I'm sorry," he said, quickly pulling his hand away. "You seem nervous. Was I too forward?"

"No," I grabbed his hand before he could retreat too far. "It's not that. I like it when you're forward." I blushed as I realized what I'd just admitted but pressed on. "I'm just... not used to this. Being hit on. People take one look at me and assume that I'm the 'aggressor' so I'm always the one who must make the first move."

The sounds of the night persisted around us as the two of us sat in silence. Crickets and frogs dueled in chorus, and a wolf howled somewhere off in the distance. I swore I could even hear moonlight dripping off the canopy above as I waited for Trent's reaction to my embarrassing confession.

Would he think me pathetic for whining about something so silly, or mock me for reacting so strongly to such simple attention?

Either option seemed like a strong possibility.

I wished I was back in the ring again. I felt confident in the middle of a fight, where my fists could solve all my problems. The moment I needed to use words, I felt apart.

I was so lost within my own thoughts that I didn't notice Trent moving closer until he was pressed right up against my side. He reached out to me again, this time resting his hand on my thigh for a brief moment and then slowly trailing his fingers upward.

"You poor thing, always being expected to do all the work. Has no one ever taken care of you?"

I watched his hand as he inched it toward my groin, instantly hard inside my pants again. Unable to speak, I merely shook my head.

Trent grinned like it was Christmas morning and every item on his list to Santa was waiting under the tree.

"Then do you mind if I'm the first one?"

This time I nodded, still unable to find my words.

With a deft twitch of his fingers, Trent undid the button of my pants and pulled down the zipper. He hesitated just long enough for me to speak up if I had changed my mind, but when my silence persisted, he slipped his hand inside my pants.

CHAPTER SIX

Trent

WHEN I FIRST saw Magnus locked inside a cage fight, I thought he was a beautifully wild force of nature. Now, as I watched him biting his lip to keep himself from moaning when I'd barely touched his cock, I could only think of one word.

Cute.

He was half-leaning against a log, half-sprawled over the dirt with his head thrown back, exposing the long line of his throat.

I stroked my hand slowly over him, barely able to move as it was trapped inside his pants.

The braid he'd tied his hair in at the beginning of the day had partially fallen apart, so at least half his hair fell in waves around his face, and the firelight made his blond locks look like polished copper. There was a small scar on his throat, just under the edge of his jaw, and I wondered if it came from another life-threatening event, or if it was from something mundane like shaving.

With Magnus, either was possible.

There was an unexpected thrill, having such a powerful man under my hand. I wasn't exactly a weakling myself. Years of weightlifting had given me plenty of strength, but I'd only ever needed to use that strength in the safety of a gym. Magnus's strength had been forged in fire and blood, riding the edge of life and death every day. In many ways, he reminded me of a wild animal, living off the land under his own power.

But even the most vicious predator needed a safe den to return to at night. I wasn't sure if I could be that den, but I could at least give him this moment of soft pleasure.

The zipper on Magnus's pants bit into my wrist, so I pulled his cock free, exposing it to the night air and my own hungry gaze. He was built stout, with a shaft that prioritized width over length. I doubted I'd be able to get my mouth around it without some practice, so I gave up on the idea of a blow job for now and just stuck to my hand.

That was something we could experiment with later.

Since we hadn't brought any supplies with us, like lube, I kept my strokes light and smeared around the pre-come leaking from the head of his cock as much as possible.

Magnus moaned, his face flushed, and the sound was swallowed by the heaviness of the night air and the crackling of the fire. I had no idea how long I'd been toying with him, but he was obviously getting close to his end, so I sped up my hand and gripped him a little harder.

When he came, he was almost completely silent. He wasn't a naturally quiet person and was biting his lip to keep his voice locked away. I recognized the symptoms of someone who'd grown up having to hide his sexuality like it was a dirty secret. Every moment of pleasure had probably been desperately hidden under the darkness of night and silence of muffled voices so no one would notice. I'd been the same way for a long time, and I hated seeing such restraint on him.

On instinct, I leaned forward and kissed him, freeing his lip from between his teeth and muffling his moans with my own mouth instead.

One of his hands grabbed the back of my head, pulling me deeper into the kiss. I didn't have long hair like him, so there wasn't as much to grab, but Magnus managed to get his fingers tangled anyway.

The kiss persisted beyond his climax. Even after he'd slumped in jelly-boned relief, we stayed locked together, gradually exploring each other.

I was eventually pulled out of the pleasure of his mouth on mine by the sting of something biting my neck. Shouting in surprise, I slapped at it, and when I pulled my hand away, I revealed the body of a squashed mosquito.

"Maybe we should take this inside," I suggested, checking my neck to make sure there wasn't a chunk of me missing. The bite had hurt a lot more than the size of the bug would imply. I'd always been particularly sensitive to bug bites, which was one of the reasons I preferred to get my exercise indoors.

"Uh, yeah," Magnus agreed, his words slurred as he was still dazed from his recent orgasm. "Just... let me douse the fire."

He'd already prepared some water from the river to use on the fire, so it was just a matter of dousing the flames and spreading out the remaining coals to make sure no hot embers remained to accidentally start a forest fire.

It was as we were opening the flap of the tent to crawl inside that Magnus seemed to come back to his senses and find his confidence, for he looped an arm around my waist and slipped two fingers into the waistband of my pants.

"You know, we'd be a lot more comfortable if we changed out of these old clothes first."

"Oh, would we," I said, smirking at him even as I pressed his hand against my hip to keep it in place.

"Oh, come on," he whined, instantly making him seem fifteen years younger. "You've seen all of me. Return the favor."

I trailed my gaze down his body. "Not all of you."

To my delight, he flushed and shifted on his feet like he was embarrassed.

"Close enough. Come on. I need to... return the favor."

He ushered me into the tent, but I stopped him and placed both hands on his shoulders, so we faced each other directly.

"You know you don't have to return anything. There's no expectation for anything."

"I know." He tugged me toward the tent again. "I want to."

The sounds of the forest around us didn't completely cut off when we zipped ourselves inside the tent. Nothing short of a soundproof room could do that.

However, a marching band could have gone by, and I wouldn't have noticed as Magnus threw off the rest of his clothes and I got a good look at all of him for the first time. There were a few more tattoos than just the one along his ribs, along with many more scars, and I was determined to get the story out of all of them. His hips were also wider than his clothing implied, balancing out his tall yet stocky frame.

I lost myself looking at him, until he tugged at the hem of my shirt. "Come on. You, too."

There wasn't much room in the tent. Even an average person would have struggled to stand up, and neither Magnus nor I qualified as average in size. I barely avoided elbowing him in the face as I removed my clothing, but we somehow managed to get ourselves comfortably laid out on the sleeping bags, completely bare and uninjured.

MAGNUS

Magnus ran his hand over my body, starting at my shoulder and moving down over my stomach toward my still hard cock. My stomach had never been flat, but I'd put on weight since I'd stopped competitively training, and now it extended over my pants more than it used to. At first, I was self-conscious about it, but Magnus seemed to enjoy the softness around my middle. He gripped at my chest, and my hips. Anywhere he could get a good handful.

"Fuck," he moaned directly against my neck. "You feel so good."

His hand finished its exploratory journey and he slipped it down between my legs to grip my arousal properly. An electric pleasure snapped across my nerves, and my arms shook as I kept myself propped up on my elbows to watch him. Magnus's strokes were slow and careful, just like mine had been, but it didn't matter. I wasn't going to last long.

It was almost embarrassing how quickly I came. One would think a man in his early forties would have a little more stamina, but no. I may as well have been a teenager again. The sight of my cock sliding through the circle of his hand, the flushed head catching against the lines of palm, had me coming in less than a minute. My arms lost their strength and I collapsed against the sleeping bags, shaking like I'd just run a marathon.

The high I felt in that moment was even better than outlifting my personal best in a competition.

"This is so much better than the first time I had sex with my last boyfriend."

I don't know why I said it. Maybe it was the endorphins still coursing through my system, or maybe I was just an idiot who never knew when to keep his mouth shut. Magnus and I hadn't even started talking about the nature of our relationship, and there I went throwing around the word "boyfriend" so casually.

Luckily, Magnus didn't look upset, or even bring up the word I'd used. He just turned to face me directly with a curious expression.

"Sounds like you've got an embarrassing story hidden away. What to share?"

I threw an arm over my eyes to block out the rest of the world. Maybe then I would be saved from my shame.

"I've got plenty of embarrassing stories, but I'll save those for later. This particular one was about a year ago. Maybe more. I don't even remember anymore. We'd only been dating for a few weeks, so it was probably too soon to call him my boyfriend, but I tend to rush into these sorts of things."

I hoped Magnus picked up the warning woven into my words so he wouldn't be surprised when I inevitably ended up rushing things with him, too.

Considering the fact that we'd gotten intimate literal days after meeting each other, maybe he had a habit of rushing things as well.

With my arm still draped over my eyes, I gave into Magnus's curiosity and explained.

"I don't like thinking about it. The sex wasn't too bad. Just the usual awkwardness you usually have with a new person whose body you don't know so well."

Come to think of it, I hadn't experienced any of that awkwardness with Magnus tonight. Sure, we hadn't gone all the way, but even a hand-job could be difficult with someone new.

I lifted my arm off my eyes just enough to peer over at Magnus. "After we finished, just as I was getting ready for a good post-coital snuggle, he asked me to leave early since he had a date to get to." A bitter laugh escaped from me, and my eyes stung as the memory of the pain I'd felt back then returned. "A date. There I was, calling him my boyfriend, and he didn't even think we were dating. It's kinda pathetic."

As if he knew exactly what I needed, Magnus reached out and pulled me closer, tucking a stray lock of sweaty hair behind my ear.

"So, what did you do?"

My ear pressed against his chest, instantly soothed by the sound of his heartbeat. "What else could I do? I left, and I never contacted him again. He probably has no idea what the problem was."

We laid in silence for a while with only the sound of our breathing to disturb us, until Magnus looked down at me with an odd smile.

"You should invite him to a cage match some time." I just looked at him confused, but his smile got even wider. "Sometimes we challenge members of the audience to try fighting us. It would be a good excuse to punch him."

My laughter echoed around the whole tent, and probably startled all the nearby wildlife. There was nothing I could do in the face of such a suggestion other than to kiss the ridiculous man beside me.

We didn't get nearly enough sleep that night.

***

Once again our day started early the next morning. We awoke with the sun, and clambered out of the tent to change, and through together a quick breakfast. There were tracks around our campsite of some large animal that had investigated us last night. We'd either been asleep or too busy to notice, but luckily, the creature had left us undisturbed since we didn't pose a threat.

If only humans could be as

considerate. Then we wouldn't be out here hiking through the woods at all and could have happily given the locket back to the police.

Once we finished packing up, the only evidence that we'd been there were the holes our tent poles had left in the ground. Everything else ended up on our backs as we started walking again.

The final destination on the map wasn't far from our campsite. If the sunlight had lasted longer, we could have investigated it yesterday, but we weren't about to go poking around the unknown in the dark.

It took us less than an hour to reach the spot we were supposedly looking for. The stream we'd camped near the night before led to a small pond at the base of a thin but beautiful waterfall. The area was completely undisturbed of any human interference and grew wild in a way that no park or maintained forest ever could.

I shielded my eyes from the morning sun to look up at the top of the waterfall.

"It's beautiful, but what are we looking for. I doubt someone made that map just to come back for the view."

Magnus studied the original map on his phone. The old paper had been too delicate to bring with us, so he'd taken several pictures of it instead.

"Well, assuming this circle is the pond, and these wavy lines are the waterfall, I think we need to go a little more this way."

He pointed toward a direction a little away from the pond. The rock wall that the waterfall fell from extended out farther than it first seemed, hidden behind the height of the trees.

We followed the wall about fifty yards and came to an area slightly higher than the rest where the trees weren't as dense. It was a perfectly hidden spot, almost invisible until we were standing right on top of it.

There, we found what the map had obviously been leading to. A structure had been carved directly into the stone wall. Only about the size of a single room, it reminded me of the mausoleums found in old graveyards. It was overgrown with vines, moss, and other plants, but the stone was still sturdy, and an open doorway stood inviting us inside.

I took a step forward, intending to see what the mausoleum held, but Magnus's hand on my shoulder brought me to a quick stop.

"Wait. Don't go near it."

"What?" I looked back at him, confused. "Why not?"

This was what we'd come here for. Surely, we wouldn't hike all this way and then not go inside.

Magnus pointed at the plants crowding around the base of the mausoleum and partially obscuring the doorway.

"See those plants?"

I observed the plants from a distance, not daring to take a single step. They were large scraggly things, a mix of both vine and bush, with small white flowers dotted among their leaves. They looked harmless at first, until I noticed the two-inch-long thorns hiding among the foliage.

"Are they dangerous?"

Magnus shook his head. "I don't know."

"Oh." I looked at the plants again. There was still some space left in the doorway. "I'm sure we could just avoid the thorns."

Before I could even think about moving, Magnus grabbed my shoulder in a death grip.

"No, Trent, you don't understand. Plants are... my thing, right? Like, I'm sure you've seen by now that I know way too much about every plant there is. If anything, I annoy people by knowing too much on the topic."

He gestured almost angrily at the plant in front of us.

"I have no idea what this is."

My mind stalled for a moment, like an engine that failed to turn over as I processed what he was saying. It was true. Magnus did seem to know everything about every plant that existed. If he didn't know what this was, then that meant...

What did it mean?

"Soooo," I eyed the plant, which somehow looked more dangerous than before now that it was officially nameless. "What do we do?"

Magnus picked up a stick from the ground and slowly approached the plant as though it might jump out and bite him.

"Until I know for sure what it is, we're not touching it."

He prodded at the plant a few times, using the stick to lift vines and turn over leaves, always keeping at least five feet between him and the plant at all times. It would have looked comedic, if the sight of his paranoia didn't send chills up my spine.

I stayed several steps behind him, not willing to get anywhere close to the plant.

"Hey, Trent," Magnus called after a moment. "Look."

With the stick he held up one branch of the plant. There, tangled among the long thorns, was a broken shoelace.

***

I sat on a boulder, watching as Magnus tried to clear the unknown plants away from the door to the mausoleum without touching them. We'd brought an emergency axe with our supplies, mostly for clearing out particularly thick underbrush since we were hiking off trail. Magnus had tied the small hand axe to a tree branch and was using it to cut away the plant from a safe distance.

It wasn't the most efficient process, but it was working. I especially enjoyed watching the muscles in his back work as he struggled with the unwieldy branch.

As I waited for Magnus to finish, which was taking a lot longer than we'd hoped, I studied the rose locket.

I couldn't explain why I brought it with me. The map had been too fragile to bring, and the coffee beans were too easily lost, so they'd both stayed back at the cabin with Brody. It had been an impulse to grab the now empty locket before leaving. If we were going to hunt down the location that this locket had led to, then it should come along for the journey.

It had been waiting a long time to fulfill its purpose, after all.

Holding the locket up to the light, I watched it sway back and forth in the air. Its chain was thin but sturdy, ensuring that the locket could never accidentally fall off.

My gaze traveled to the broken shoelace that sat in a sealed baggie beside me. The first thing Magnus had done after investigating the unnamed plant, was to carefully extract the shoelace without touching it and seal it away in a Ziploc bag, along with a few cuttings from the plant to be examined later.

The shoelace was thin and black, made for a dress shoe rather than a hiking one. It was no wonder the string had broken when someone had gone stomping around out here.

"Hey, Magnus," I called, still staring at the shoestring in the clear bag.

"Hmm?" Magnus looked up from his battle with the unnamed plant. "What's up?"

"Something just occurred to me." I held up the baggie with the shoelace for him to see. "If this shoelace belongs to Deputy Hillard, like we suspect, then that means he was out here long before he approached me the first time. Possibly before the coffin was even dug up."

Breathing heavily with sweat staining his blond hair a darker color around the edges, Magnus leaned against his jerry-rigged pruning axe.

"Yeah. What about it?"

"Well," I sighed, putting down the shoelace to turn the locket over in my fingers again. The locket that had contained the map to find this place. "That means he already knew where this place was. So why try to steal the locket if he didn't need the map?"

Magnus also stared at the shoelace and locket for a moment, before shaking his head and returning to his task.

"I have no idea. We don't know enough about anything to even begin to guess what's going on. Let's just focus on finding a way in here without hurting ourselves and hope that it has some answers."

It took another hour before Magnus managed to get enough of the plant cleared out so that we could safely pass through the door. Plenty of the plant remained, standing like thorny sentries on either side of the door, and I couldn't help but hold my breath as we passed into structures shadowed interior.

It wasn't as dark as it looked from the outside, thanks to thin windows carved into the walls to let in some sunlight, but it still took a moment for our eyes to adjust so we could see the room around us. The structure had been carved right into the stone wall, rather than built brick by brick, so there were no seams or grout lines like there would be in typical stone buildings. The walls were as smooth as glass and had clearly been constructed with a great amount of care, despite the lack of artistic detail.

This was not a place that had been

built on a whim. A lot of care had been put into it, and even the very air around us seemed to pulse with a warm feeling.

At the center of the mausoleum stood three nearly identical structures. No plants grew on these, but I still approached the nearest one with caution. The room around us was very plain, and I wondered if that was because whoever built it had dedicated all their artistic talent to these three structures. They were intricately carved. Not a single inch lay unadorned, except for a few inches near the top where words had been carved.

A thick layer of dust and cobwebs lay over the top of the structure, which I delicately brushed away to read the words beneath.

Rose Milford.

Checking the other structures revealed similar names carved into the stone there as well.

Lisianthus Milford.

Poppy Milford.

"They're graves," Magnus said just as the same thought occurred to me.

"Old graves," I added, tracing the letters of the nearest name. "Milford? That's the name of the family that founded Emberwood, isn't it."

"Yeah," Magnus agreed, though he wasn't looking at the names. "Our property used to belong to a man named Ben Milford, who I'm told was the last Milford decedent. These three sisters must be his ancestors."

"Sisters?" I asked, stepping closer to see what had drawn his attention. "What makes you so sure they were sisters?"

He was inspecting the carvings all over the stone crypt, using his phone to take pictures of the designs that looked like flowering vines.

Plants.

Of course.

Magnus stood up from where he'd been crouching at the side of the crypt and tapped the carved design.

"Isn't it obvious. I'd guess they were even triplets. Themed names seem like the kind of thing you'd do with triplets."

"Themed names?"

With wide, confused eyes, Magnus pointed at the names written on the lids.

"Rose, Lisianthus, and Poppy. They're all flowers."

"Oh." I looked at the names again. Each structure was carved with a slightly different flower theme, which I assumed matched their names. "I recognized Rose and Poppy, but I've never heard of Lisianthus."

"Yeah, it's not as common." Magnus ran his hand over what was probably a Lisianthus flower. "A lot of people mistake them for roses. They look very similar, although the Lisianthus is a bit more..." He made a vague gesture like he was trying to pull the description out of the air. "Frilly."

His face twisted into a grimace, obviously not liking the word he'd chosen, but looking at the carvings, I thought it fit.

"Wait a minute." I pulled out the locket again. "Rose."

It couldn't be a coincidence that the locket that led us here was designed to look like a rose as well.

"You think it used to belong to her?" Magnus asked, looking between the locket and the rose covered crypt. "I remember you saying the journal also had a rose engraved on it. Maybe all three objects belonged to her."

"No," I quickly said as I recalled my first inspection of the items found inside the mysterious coffin. It seemed like so long ago.

Had only three days really passed since then?

MAGNUS

Shaking away my confused perception of time, I grabbed Magnus's shoulder with excitement.

"Since the art style was different, I thought they were both roses made by two different people. But maybe it wasn't a rose. Maybe it was something that looked similar to a rose."

We both glanced toward the carved Lisianthus flowers. I would need to see the journal again to know for sure, but my instincts told me I was right.

Magnus stepped back so he could see all three crypts at once. "Three sisters. Three objects. It would make sense. So, you think the key had some sort of poppy design on it that we didn't notice?"

"It's likely. When I inspected the objects, I was focused on age and craftsmanship. I wasn't looking for themes in the artwork. But that still leaves one question? If there was an object for each sister in that coffin, then whose body was buried there?"

None of the three crypts looked disturbed. Dust and spiderwebs covered them all equally, but that didn't rule out the option that someone had tampered with them.

The thought of it turned my stomach. These three sisters had been laid together with such care. For someone to come along and steal one of them, permanently separating them after death, was heartbreaking.

Needing to know the answer, I grabbed the lid of the nearest crypt and shoved, intending to see if any of them were empty. To my surprise, the lid didn't budge, and all I managed to do was nearly wrench my shoulder out of the socket.

"Woah," Magnus called as he pulled me away from the crypts. "Hold on. Despite what the movies always show, you can't just open one of these things. They're solid stone and very heavy. Plus, they're often sealed shut to stop people from tampering with them." His gaze flickered up and down my body, his pupils dilating a bit as a smirk played on his lips. "Even a competitive weightlifter can't just open these things. We'll need special tools."

I deflated like a balloon that had escaped someone's hands to fly around the room before falling limp and empty on the floor. All my energy escaped me at once, and I practically wilted on the spot.

"Oh. I didn't know that. So, we'll have to go all the way back, get the right tools, then hike all the way out here again?"

That would take days at least.

"Come on." Magnus steered me toward the door with a comforting arm around my shoulder. "There's not much more we can do here with the supplies we brought. The sooner we get going, the sooner we'll be back. Plus, maybe we won't need to open the crypts at all. The police may have identified the body by now."

"Assuming they would even tell us if they did," I grumbled, but I followed him.

We'd spent so much time trying to get into the mausoleum, that there was no way for us to make it all the way back to town by the end of the day. We went as far as we could with what sunlight remained, but inevitably had to make camp again.

It wasn't as peaceful as the first night, as we were both impatient to return, and we were too tired to do anything other than sleep. Yet, it was still comforting to drift off with Magnus pressed up against me and with his arm thrown across my chest.

I didn't want to admit it yet, not even to myself, but I could easily imagine sleeping like that every night.

***

The next morning, we were up and

packed even before the sun rose, and started traveling again as soon as the first rays of light breached the canopy. We didn't talk much, focused on traveling as quickly as we could with single-minded determination.

Because we left so early and didn't have to cover the entire distance in one day, it was only mid-morning when the first sight of Magnus and Brody's property came into view.

The first thing I saw was Magnus's garden, and the fresh patch of dirt that we had prepared together.

"Home sweet home." I grinned over at Magnus, only to find him scowling instead.

"That's... strange," he said, scanning the area like he was looking for something, and even checking behind him. "Usually the dogs are patrolling the perimeter. They should have noticed us before we even got here."

"Maybe they're inside the house," I suggested, trying to remain hopeful.

Yet, Magnus dashed my hopes by shaking his head.

"Not during the day. They're always outside. Had to build their own dog houses, because they refused to come inside, even during bad weather."

Before I could offer any more reassurance, we were interrupted by the unmistakable sound of a gunshot echoing across the clearing.

"Brody!" Magnus shouted as he dumped his gear on the ground and took off running.

I threw my bag next to his and followed him, always just a few steps behind.

CHAPTER SEVEN

Magnus

MY FEET POUNDED against the ground, propelling me forward as fast as possible, yet it still wasn't fast enough. I would have teleported if I could. As my heart pounded in my ears and my breathing rattled heavily in my lungs, I could think of only one thing.

Brody.

I should have known better. Should have recognized the sound of the gun. If I had, I wouldn't have been surprised with I rounded the side of Brody's house and found him standing on his porch with his gun braced against his shoulder and his finger on the trigger.

"Mag," he said calmly without lifting his eye from the sight of his gun. "You're back already? Where's your boyfriend?"

A moment later Trent also rounded the house and dug his heels into the ground to bring himself to a sudden stop as he took in the scene.

"Carlton?"

At first, I was confused by the sound of Trent's voice speaking an unexpected name. But then I followed the point of Brody's gun to another figure standing in our yard a few dozen feet away.

I recognized the face immediately. I'd seen it every time I'd gone to the hardware store.

Carlton Thornley.

It wasn't that long ago I'd regularly made a fool of myself just to talk to him.

Yet, since the mystery of the coffin found on the property and Trent had entered my life, I'd completely forgotten about him. I regretted that now that he was on our property. The man looked terrified. His handsome face was wide with panic and his expression had fallen slack, like his brain had temporarily stopped working. I almost felt bad for him, except it was clear he must have come with ill intentions based on the way Brody kept a gun pointed at him, and our dogs growled as they surrounded him, keeping the man from going anywhere.

"Please, don't kill me," Carlton begged, falling to his knees. "I don't mean any harm."

That was when I noticed the rip in his pants right across his outer thigh. It was too thin for me to see the skin beneath, but blood had stained the cloth around the tear. I recognized Brody's handiwork. The shot I'd heard earlier must have grazed Carlton's leg.

Brody was too good a marksman to miss at such close range. The leg injury had been intentional. It was a warning shot. The next time Brody pulled that trigger, the bullet was going right between Carlton's eyes.

"No harm?" Brody said even as his gun never wavered. "That's hard to believe when I caught you trying to break into my house with a knife."

Looking around, I quickly located the knife in question. It lay on the porch near the front door, glinting in the midmorning sun as if trying to draw attention to itself. It wasn't a machete or anything too dangerous, but it also wasn't a simple pocketknife either. A knife like that could easily kill someone.

"No, it's not like that," Carlton shouted, then flinched when Onyx started growling louder. "I just brought the knife for the lock on the door. I wasn't planning on harming anyone."

Trent stepped up next to me, his presence a comforting warmth against my side. "So, what were you planning?"

Whatever had brought Carlton to us, he obviously hadn't known about Trent's involvement, because he looked shocked at the sight of the other man.

"Trent? What the hell are you doing here?"

Trent merely crossed his arms, looking unimpressed. "I was invited. I don't think you can say the same. Now, answer your own question. What the hell are you doing here?"

Brody's gun creaked as he held it higher against his shoulder. "Committing suicide. That's what." Carlton moved as if he was about to stand up, but froze when Brody cocked his gun again, priming the next bullet. "Don't move. You'll die a lot quicker if I get a clean shot."

"Hold on," I called, holding up both

hands to ask everyone for silence. "No one's killing anyone." Carlton opened his mouth with a relieved look on his face, obviously about to thank me, but I cut him off. "Yet. That option might be back on the table depending on your answers. So, first question. Are you here because of the locket?"

I expected him to deny it, and assumed I'd be able to tell by his eyes whether he was lying. Instead, all I got was a look of confusion.

"A locket? Is that what you found in the coffin?"

Brody's gun finally lowered from his eye just enough for him to peer over the edge of the sight at Carlton. "You came to rob us without even knowing what you were looking for?"

As Carlton's mouth gaped like a fish, struggling to find an answer, Trent leaned over to whisper to me.

"I don't think he actually knows

anything about what's going on?"

"It would explain why he was surprised to find you here," I whispered back. "If he was specifically targeting the locket, he'd only be looking for it here because he knew you brought it to us."

Something wasn't adding up. So, taking a chance, I stepped out in front of the house and approached Carlton. Even without looking I could feel the intensity of Brody's gaze as he raised his gun back to his eye, ready to fire at any sign of a threat.

Onyx and Indigo stopped growling when I reached them, but Pip never let down his guard. The little Chihuahua's eyes were locked on Carlton, even as I offered the man a hand to stand up.

"You're gonna have to explain what's going on. If you didn't know about the locket, why did you try to break into our place?"

Carlton accepted my hand and

clambered to his feet, but quickly let go and cast a nervous glance over at Brody and Trent.

"I heard you found something in the coffin you dug up," Carlton explained. "It's all anyone can talk about, but the police aren't telling us what was specifically found. There's a rumor going around that it was something from the Milford sisters, and that the police let you keep it."

An image of the three crypts in the mausoleum sprang to mind, and a part of me wished I was back in the woods where everything seemed less complicated.

Did everyone in town know about the Milford sisters' mausoleum?

If so, why had the map to their final resting place been so well hidden?

While I struggled to think of what to say, Trent covered up my indecision and called out to Carlton.

"The police didn't leave anything here.

Why would you think that? And even if they had, why would you try to steal it?"

Technically, nothing Trent said was a lie. The police hadn't left the locket with us. They'd left it with Trent. He then just so happened to bring it to us later.

Glancing over my shoulder, I caught Trent's eye, and a knowing smirk passed between us.

Carlton, meanwhile, started backing away from me one slow step at a time.

"It was just a rumor. You're right. I shouldn't have listened to such things. I'll just go, and we can forget about all this."

"Hold it," Brody called before Carlton could take another step. "You're not going anywhere until you answer our questions. Take one more step and I'll put another hole in you."

Carlton immediately clamped his hand down over the wound on his thigh. It was barely bleeding, definitely meant more to scare than to harm, but the sight of his blood seemed to unnerve him, and he started shaking.

"Y-you can't d-do that. I'm n-not a threat now."

The first shot could be considered self-defense since Carlton had trespassed on our property with a weapon, but anything we did to him now that he was unarmed and no longer attacking us would be considered excessive. Yet, Brody never lowered his weapon. In fact, if anything, his grip on the weapon tightened.

"Without knowing why you're here, there's no way for us to know for sure that you're not a threat. Besides..."

The grin Brody gave Carlton chased away all traces of softness from his face and left no room for doubt about his lethality as a soldier.

"There're no cameras out here to prove what happened. As far as anyone will know, you broke in, I shot you in self-defense. End of story."

I'd known Brody long enough to understand that he was bluffing. While the man never hesitated to pull the trigger when necessary, killing a citizen would always be a last resort and this was far from a last resort situation.

However, Trent didn't know Brody as well, and I could see the fear in his eyes as he glanced at the gun. I tried to catch his gaze to give him some hint that everything would be okay, but it didn't work since I couldn't risk being too obvious and giving away Brody's bluff.

"Y-you can't," Carlton repeated.

The end of Brody's gun stayed steadfast.

"You really want to take that chance."

Even from a distance, I could see the wheels turning in Trent's head. He was thinking about stepping in, but then he finally looked in my direction. The moment our eyes met, he seemed to calm down, and the fear left his expression.

The same was not true for Carlton. He glanced between the three of us, finding nothing but a threat in all directions. He even glanced at our dogs, as if he might find help there, but when he shuffled back another step, Pip took that as the sign to attack and latched onto his pant leg, violently shaking the cloth between his teeth.

For a moment, it seemed like he might try to remove the dog, but then I cleared my throat to get his attention and gave him a very clear "don't you dare" look.

Pip was left alone to wage war against the cuffs of the man's pants.

"Fine," Carlton said, caving under the pressure from all sides. He wrung his hands and stared at the ground as he spoke, but his voice had at least stopped shaking. "I overheard my family talking about what was found hidden along with the body in the coffin. We were hoping it was something left behind by Rose

Milford. We didn't know what had been found, but this is Milford property. If there was anything from Rose Milford to discover, it would be here."

The man had become a pile of nervous twitches, and stumbled over his feet twice, nearly kicking Pip in the process.

I picked up the little dog before he got hurt and set him down next to Indigo where he could continue to growl at our intruder in peace.

"Okay. That explains why you didn't know what you were looking for, but not why you were looking for it in the first place. Who's Rose Milford to you and why do you care about finding anything from her?"

I narrowed my eyes as Carlton clenched his fists, but all the man did was straighten his spine and stand a little taller.

"Rose Milford killed someone from my family."

He apparently expected this declaration to get more of a reaction, because when he was met with three blank looks of indifference, his moment of confidence faded.

"Okay," I said, and glanced again at Trent to see of the other man had any idea what Carlton was talking about. Yet, Trent looked just as confused as I felt, and I was left trying to navigate the conversation on my own. "I'm sorry to hear that. I guess. Why does it matter?"

"Because..." Carlton spread out both hands in a vague shrug, like even he didn't know what to do with his own answer. "Most people in town think of the Milford sisters as saints. Like God himself dropped them on this earth. They refuse to believe my family when we claim that Rose Milford killed a member of our family."

With Brody armed and ready at my back, I felt safe enough to drop my face into my palm in a show of exasperation.

"Again, I repeat, why does that matter? This would have happened around a hundred and twenty-five years ago, right? What does it matter now?"

Carlton managed to take one aggressive step toward me before he remembered the gun pointed at him and immediately backed off again. "It matters because we could never prove it. My ancestor, Jacob Thornley, was a decent man, and she killed him in cold blood. His body was never discovered, and we were never able to put him to rest. It's haunted my family ever since, like a shame we could never get rid of. Now a body is discovered on Milford property, a body that could very well be my ancestor, but the police aren't telling us anything. They won't even tell us about the objects found with the body. So, I thought..."

"You thought you'd come here and try to uncover some evidence on your own," I finished for him. Sighing again, I pinched the bridge of my nose to ward off a headache. "Look, Carlton. You must know that what you're doing is insane right now, right? Like, certifiably insane. The body we found hasn't been identified as your ancestor, and you said it yourself that there was no evidence that Rose Milford killed him. With no body and no proof, how do you even know he was murdered?"

"He was," Carlton grumbled, though he couldn't look me in the eye. "My family knows it. We just haven't been able to prove it."

"Well, do you even know why she would have killed him?"

He didn't answer me, but his silence was enough, and I just sighed again.

"Of course not. Look, I'm sure you're just trying to help your family out, but this is not the way to do it. Breaking into someone else's property like this is dangerous." I looked over at Brody, who had lowered his gun but not dropped it entirely. "Very dangerous. So, why don't you just leave, and like you said earlier, we can forget this happened. All right?"

It took some more convincing, but I eventually managed to herd Carlton off our property and send him on his way back home empty handed and disappointed. He didn't even bother asking for his knife back as he walked off into the woods toward the car he'd apparently hidden at the end of the road.

I watched him until he was fully out of sight, then ran both hands through my hair with an aggravated groan.

"Ugh, I can't believe I used to have a crush on him."

"Is that so?"

I jumped a foot in the air and turned to face Trent who had managed to sneak up beside me while I was distracted.

"It's, um... I mean..."

Trent raised an eyebrow at my stuttering, and the coy smirk that twisted his mouth nearly made my knees give out on the spot.

"You never told me I have competition," Trent said, looking off in the direction that Carlton had disappeared. "I think I could beat him. Unless you're into stupid. I don't think I could match that."

I was saved from having to answer when Brody joined us. He'd put his gun back in its place on the rack by the door, but I could tell he was still on edge from the way he kept one hand hovering near the knife holstered on his belt.

"So, does anyone want to tell me who the hell the Milford sisters are?"

***

Letting Carlton leave may have been my idea, but hours later I regretted my decision. No matter what I did, I couldn't shake the itching feeling under my skin, like there was a snake hissing in the grass just beneath my feet but I couldn't see it and didn't know which way to step.

Unfortunately, Carlton hadn't committed any crime other than a minor act of trespassing. Under normal circumstances it would barely be worth pursuing, and with our suspicions about the local law enforcement still raised, we weren't going to contact them. We had no choice but to let Carlton go and hope that Brody's good aim had been enough to scare him away permanently.

The rest of the day was spent telling Brody about the Milford sisters and their mausoleum that the map had led us to. That discussion alone took a few hours, especially since we kept getting sidetracked with speculations that we couldn't prove. From there, we also spent time debating the merits of going back to the mausoleum.

We could open the three crypts to see

if the bodies of the sisters were there, but what would it accomplish?

It wouldn't prove the identity of the body we'd found, and after hearing Carlton's suspicions about the body, I doubted it was one of the sisters anyway.

As day turned into night, my mind raced with thoughts of coffee beans and shoelaces.

What was the point of the coffee beans hidden in the locket?

Why were so many people focused on the three sisters' mausoleum?

Why had Rose Milford supposedly killed Carlton's ancestor, Jacob Thornley?

If the body on our property wasn't one of the three sisters, why had their items been buried there?

These questions plagued me long after the sun had gone down, and I was once again sitting on the edge of my own bed.

"I can practically hear you thinking from here," Trent said as he stood in front of me, running one hand through my loose hair.

I sighed and leaned against his palm. "I just don't understand what's going on. We keep finding more pieces of the puzzle, but none of them seem to fit together into any sort of cohesive image."

Trent's second hand joined his first and both started rubbing at my scalp, relieving the headache that had started to form.

"Don't worry so much. We'll figure it out. And so what if we don't? All this stuff happened a hundred and twenty-five years ago. Even if we never figure out the secret, it won't affect us."

His fingers were bliss, chasing away my headache almost immediately. I couldn't help moaning in disappointment when his massage stopped. Not wanting to lose his presence so soon, I pulled him down so he was sitting next to me on the bed.

"Maybe it won't affect us, but secrets are powerful things. I'm worried about what the people who are affected by the secret might do if they think we're a threat. There's nothing more dangerous than a human who feels threatened."

Trent leaned closer until our foreheads almost touched and I could feel the heat from his breath against my skin.

"I assume you're speaking from experience, but I'm curious which side you were on."

I barely heard his words, distracted by the feeling of his hand settling against my hip. I could tell he'd asked me a question, but my hormone-soaked brain couldn't muster more than a confused "Huh?"

Trent's laugh was more air than sound, but it still made a shiver run over my skin.

"Your experience with threatening people," he explained. "I'm curious if that comes as the threatener or the threatenee."

"Uh, both," I said, right before choking on my own spit when he slid his hand up my hip to dip under the hem of my shirt. "Do you... do you really want to talk about my combat history right now?"

"No, not really."

He was so close his lips brushed mine with every word, yet just when I thought he was about to kiss me, he unexpectedly pulled back.

"Unless..."

I sat there, frozen, not sure what to do with the sudden distance between us.

"Unless what?"

"Unless this isn't what you want." Trent stared down at his own hands, which were now twisted together in his lap. "I mean, we haven't really talked about our expectations for anything, so maybe I misread things."

I finally managed to snap out of my stupor and shook my head, causing my hair to fly around my shoulders as I stared at him in bewilderment. "What are you talking about?"

"This." He gestured between the two of us. "I'm here, in your bed, practically throwing myself at you, but you don't really seem happy about it. What we did together while we were out in the woods was great, but I can understand if things are different now that we're back. It can be like Vegas. What happens in the woods stays in the woods. I won't mind."

When it finally dawned on me what he was saying, I wasn't sure whether to slap myself or kiss him.

Trent couldn't read my mind. He had no idea how giddy I felt every time he touched me. From his perspective, I'd just been sitting here like an idiot, too caught up in my own head to respond to his obvious flirting.

I really wanted to punch myself for putting that insecure look on his face, but instead, I grabbed his shoulders and shoved him down on the bed so I was kneeling over him.

"I don't want to keep you a secret," I said, straddling him so he could feel exactly how excited I was by his sheer proximity. "Brody already knows about my sexuality, and I really don't care what anyone else thinks."

Trent's dark eyes stared up at me, wide and glittering with a mix of emotions. "Oh, good. I was afraid that... well, we never discussed if you were out to anyone else, and if you were even interested in a relationship. It wouldn't be the first time someone wanted to keep me a secret."

"Fuck no," I declared, then flinched when I realized I'd practically shouted in his face. "I'm sorry if I made you feel like that. It's definitely not what I want. I just... most of my experience in the past has been quick fucks and one-night stands. I'm not really sure what to do when someone wants to stay."

He threaded his hand back into my hair, cupping the side of my face with more tenderness than I felt I deserved.

"I want to stay."

The hand in my hair pulled me forward and I followed.

"Good. Because I want you to stay, too."

This time when we kissed, I made sure to respond, pouring all the passion I felt into the embrace so there could be no question about my feelings.

Trent gasped against my lips and responded in kind, matching my heat and driving us both higher until every place we touched felt like we were melting together.

I pulled back from the kiss just long enough to catch a breath, then dove right back in, never parting for long enough to let the heat between us die, even a little.

There was no telling how much time had passed as our hands and mouths wandered, but by the end of it, both our clothes ended up on the floor and we were tangled together on the bed without any barriers.

Trent's hand gripped my chest, squeezing and kneading the muscles he found there as he nipped a line of fire down my throat.

"Please tell me you've got stuff here."

"What?" I gasped, barely paying attention to what he was saying.

To my dismay, Trent stopped and leaned back to look me in the eye. "Protection. Please tell me you've got protection and stuff here, because I think I will die if I can't fuck you right now."

"Ugh... yeah. Hang on."

I reached toward my nightstand with clumsy, chaotic gestures. Somehow, I managed to knock several books to the floor and nearly pulled the drawer straight out of the nightstand in my frantic searching, but a moment later, I dropped my spoils on the bed next to us.

The condoms were perhaps older than they should have been, I'd never checked the expiration date, and the bottle of lubricant was half empty, but it would still work.

Trent ended up leaning over me, one leg thrown over my hips as if to pin me down and make sure I didn't go anywhere.

It was such a silly thought. Of course, I wasn't going anywhere.

Where else would I want to be?

He reached for the condoms and lubricant, inspecting them for a moment before deeming them good enough. The quality of the supplies I could provide caused my cheeks to blush in embarrassment, and I vowed to go to the store in the morning. In my defense, it had been a long time since I invited anyone over, and usually the lubricant was only meant for the aid of my own hand.

It was such a familiar move, watching Trent spreading the lube over his own fingers before reaching down between my legs. I'd seen other men do it before and done it plenty of times myself for other partners, but somehow it was different with him. I was nervous in a way I hadn't been since I was a virgin blindly navigating my first sexual experience.

I may as well have stayed a virgin all my life for all the good my previous experiences did me. The moment I felt Trent's hand brush against my ass, I jumped as if struck by static shock.

"Nervous?" Trent asked. That singular word was laced with laughter.

At first, I was too afraid to look up at him, but when I did, I found only warmth in his eyes.

"I shouldn't be, but..." I looked away

again. "Somehow, this feels different. Because I know you'll still be there tomorrow, it matters more. I can't just walk away if it doesn't go well."

He nodded, considering my words with a seriousness that didn't belong in such a heated moment.

"Sleeping with someone for the first time can be awkward. We're still learning each other, after all. So, I won't judge if your performance is underwhelming. However..." He leaned closer, and the hand that wasn't currently gripping my ass wrapped around my cock. "I don't think that'll be a problem."

His palm was warm as he started stroking me, and the calluses on his fingers, still left over from his competition days, created a pleasant friction. I gripped tight to the sheet beneath me, throwing my head back as each stroke of his hand sent pleasure jolting along my body like an overcharged electrical line.

I would have finished right there if he had kept it up, but after only a few strokes, he released me. The wail of despair that escaped my lips sounded like something that belonged in a horror movie, and I grabbed his wrist as I desperately tried to pull him back to me.

Trent kissed me, sweet and brief. "Nope. Not yet. I've got other plans for you."

His fingers pressed against me again, this time applying just enough pressure for one of them to slip inside.

I breathed deeply and forced myself to relax against the intrusion. No matter how many times I'd done this before, it always felt a little strange at first. However, it took barely any time at all for Trent's finger to hit just the right spot, sending a wave of pleasure over me, and reminding me why I loved this so much.

After that, it took almost no time at all for Trent to finish preparing me. I was eager for him. Desperate in a way that I rarely was with previous partners. A second and a third finger quickly followed the first, and the stretch inside me was nothing but a pleasant, taunting ache.

"Hurry up," I begged as I clung to him. "I'm not delicate. You don't need to be so gentle. I can take more."

"I'm sure you can," he mumbled against my throat as he pressed kisses over my heated skin. "But it's our first time. I want it to be perfect."

"I don't need perfect." I raked my hands against his shoulders like claws in a frantic bid to pull him closer. "I just need you."

My words must have greatly affected him, for his mouth molded against mine so suddenly, and with such heat, that our teeth clashed together. I didn't even mind the pain since he continued to kiss me at the same time. When he deemed me ready, he pulled his fingers free and quickly rolled one of the condoms over himself before positioning his hips between my legs. I could feel every inch of his body. All the hard and soft lines of him came together into an intoxicating weight pressing down on me, pinning me to the bed as he lined himself up.

No more words passed between us, but our kiss ended just long enough for us to look into each other's eyes. Everything we needed to say was exchanged in that look.

Then, without hesitation, Trent pressed inside me.

My body struggled to accommodate him, and the stretch of inner muscles made me groan. Trent was gentle, yet unyielding as he slowly claimed me inch my inch.

I wrapped both arms and legs around him, keeping him as close to me as possible until he was finally, blissfully, all the way inside. We were as connected as two people could possibly be, yet it wasn't enough. I wanted more.

I clenched my legs around his waist and threaded my hands through his hair. "Come on, baby. Don't tease. Let me have it."

Trent laughed as he kissed me again, then nipped at my bottom lip. The unexpected spark of pain distracted me just enough that I wasn't prepared when he suddenly pulled his hips back and slammed inside again. Every nerve in my body seemed to explode at once, and I shouted as he continued thrusting inside me.

His pace was ruthless, but never quite fast enough to push me over the edge. I begged and pleaded for more. Harder. Faster. Anything. Usually, I wasn't so talkative in bed, but I couldn't seem to silence myself as Trent pushed just a little deeper and just a little harder with each thrust.

His broad shoulders easily held up

against my desperate grip, keeping me steady even as he took me apart.

In the back of my mind, I noticed the sound of the headboard hitting the wall and was grateful that the furniture was so sturdy. I wouldn't have wanted to explain the broken bed to Brody in the morning.

Eventually, Trent sped up, and I nearly wept in relief as I felt the edge of my climax finally crawling closer. His movements lost their rhythm, becoming chaotic and frantic. The obscene sound of skin against skin echoed around the room, drowning out our shared moans. Every inch of me shook, and I lost control of my limbs, clinging to him with all the strength I had.

The orgasm hit me like lightning and white lights danced in front of my eyes as I shuddered through the pleasure. My stomach was coated in the results of my release, hot and wet against my skin, and lubricating the slide of our bodies against each other as Trent's pace never slowed.

His arms tightened around me hard enough to crush the air from my lungs. Then, with one final thrust, deeper and harder than anything before, his whole body went stiff. The condom he wore meant I felt nothing from his climax other than a slight heat inside me. As much as I understood the necessity, I hated it. It would have been so much more satisfying to feel him filling me, leaving me stained inside and out.

I'd never had a partner that I trusted enough to forego protection, so I had no idea what it truly felt like. My curiosity was piqued. Someday, if everything with Trent worked out, we could experiment without protection in the future.

Maybe.

For a long time afterward, we simply lay there, chests heaving against each other and sweat slowly cooling against our skin as we calmed down. Trent brushed away a lock of my hair that had stuck to the spit leaking from the corner of my mouth before kissing me. This time, the kiss was slow, just a soft press of lips with very little heat. It felt more like a reminder that he was there, still with me, than an act of passion.

The sweet gesture soothed the last of my trembling, and a heavy lethargy settled over my limbs. Eventually, we'd have to leave the bed to clean ourselves up, but for a few more minutes we continued to lie there, messy and content.

CHAPTER EIGHT

Trent

AFTER SLEEPING IN a different place for the last four nights, I'd lost all sense of where I was when I woke up. I recognized the ceiling, I'd slept under it before, but the angle was wrong.

My blurry confusion only lasted until I rolled over onto my side and came face to face with Magnus lying only a few inches away. His hair was spread out over his pillow in messy golden waves, tickling my cheek where the tendrils reached toward me.

Right.

We were back at Magnus's house, and last night we'd finally gone all the way.

It was so strange. I'd never been the most confident person in relationships, usually just going along with whatever my partner wanted. At first sight, Magnus had seemed exactly like the kind of guy I'd need to kowtow to, and I'd been okay with that.

Yet, somehow, I'd found myself falling into the role of the seducer. It was so easy to be confident around Magnus that I never questioned it until I was pinning him down, and then I was enjoying myself too much to stop.

I still didn't want to stop. I didn't want anything about our current dynamic to change. It was odd, but good.

Magnus was still deeply asleep, so I slipped out of the bed and headed for the bathroom to shower. We'd taken the time to quickly clean up last night, but I still felt a bit grimy around the edges.

On the way out of the room, I stole some clothes from Magnus's closet and didn't think twice about it until I was halfway through my shower.

Standing under the raining water, it hit me. I'd gotten comfortable in Magnus's home very quickly; so much so that I didn't even hesitate to steal his clothes or monopolize his bathroom. These were the kinds of things I'd never felt comfortable doing until I was at least months into a relationship, yet here I was, less than a week in and already making myself at home.

It didn't help that Magnus's home was very comfortable. He and Brody had designed it themselves, and since they were both larger men, everything had been sized for them.

Well, it wasn't really Magnus's house. Technically, the place belonged only to

Brody, and Magnus was living there while his own house was built, but since they had designed it together, the sentiment remained the same.

I loved my grandparents, but they had both been average in size, and the apartment over the shop I'd inherited from them reflected that. Being able to shower without ducking my head to fit under the showerhead or keep my elbows pinned against my side to avoid knocking them against the wall was a novel experience. I would miss it when I eventually returned home.

I stilled my hands in the process of washing my hair, foam dripping down my temple and into my ear.

Damn.

I would eventually have to go back home. Truthfully, I probably should have already. There was no reason for me to stay here. The security system in my shop and apartment was more than sufficient to fend off anyone who tried to break in, and my building was in the center of town. If I did get into trouble, I'd have plenty of neighbors to rely on.

However, none of those neighbors were as good in a fight as Magnus, or as good with a gun as Brody. No matter how good my own security system was, I was still safer here. After all, we still didn't know specifically why Deputy Hillard tried to break into my place, or what he intended, so staying here was the best option for now.

I started moving my hands again, returning to the task of my shower. I even started humming to myself, happy that I could put off the thought of returning home a little longer.

Although, I would probably have to fetch some of my own clothes eventually. Magnus's clothes worked, but we were built a little differently, so they didn't fit as well as my own. As I walked down the stairs to the kitchen, I could feel them pulling tight across my thighs, and the neckline of the shirt was higher than I preferred.

Breakfast was already waiting in the kitchen, laid out on plates and ready to be reheated. Magnus's was still asleep upstairs, so Brody must have prepared the food. It was later than I'd thought, almost midmorning, and the food had obviously been made some time ago. Through the window, I could see Brody out in the yard, doing something I couldn't discern with a stack of lumber.

I made a note to thank him later as I sat down to eat.

My thoughts were still filled with the memories of everything we'd discovered over the last few days, and my developing relationship with Magnus, that before I knew it, I'd finished eating and had spent several hours sitting by the window sipping a now cold cup of coffee. The sound of the clock chiming the hour shocked me out of my contemplation.

A grandfather clock stood in the corner of the room. The antique salesman that had taken permanent roost in my heart couldn't help evaluating it, and while it had the look of something old, it was actually a new creation that had just been made to look old. The clock called out eleven strikes of its bell, alerting me to the fact that it was already almost midday.

Breakfast was far behind us now, and lunch was quickly approaching. Yet, Magnus still hadn't come down.

Was he still sleeping?

Was he unwell?

We'd had an exhausting night last night, so maybe he was just tired, but a part of me couldn't help but worry that I'd done something wrong and hurt him.

Telling myself to calm down, I set my coffee mug in the sink and headed upstairs to check on Magnus.

The bed was empty, as was the bathroom, and I knew he hadn't gone outside since I'd been able to see both the front and back door of the house from where I'd been sitting downstairs. While the house was comfortably large, there weren't that many individual rooms. My search didn't last long, and I soon found Magnus sitting behind a desk in a small office. The desk in front of him was covered in several open books, which he was flipping through with one hand while typing away on a laptop with the other.

I knocked my knuckles against the door frame to announce my presence before stepping into the room. "Magnus? What are you doing?"

"Hmm?"

Magnus didn't immediately look away from the book when he addressed me, and barely seemed to be aware of my presence. I wasn't until I stood directly before the desk that he finally looked up, and his attention snapped away from the book toward me with the force of a broken rubber band.

"Oh, sorry Trent. I was just looking some stuff up."

The office only had one chair, so I sat on the edge of the desk, once again glad for the strong custom-built furniture that could easily hold my weight.

"Looking up what?"

He tapped several different pictures in the books he'd been looking through. It was absolutely no surprise that all the books were about plants.

"I was trying to look up that strange plant surrounding the mausoleum."

Casting a second glance at the books, the plants shown in the pictures did have some similarities to the one we'd seen, but even my untrained eye could tell that none of them were exactly right.

"Still bothered that you couldn't identify the plant?"

"Yes." Magnus angrily flipped through a few more pages, each one resembling the unknown plant a little less. "I know everything that grows naturally in this area, so I thought maybe it was some sort of exotic import that someone brought it for decoration. But I've already been searching for hours, and I can't identify it. None of these plants are right. If I hadn't seen it with my own eyes, I'd say this plant doesn't exist."

"You think the plant is something unidentified?"

Magnus slammed all the books and the laptop shut, then pinched the bridge of his nose. "Either that, or my research skills aren't as good as I thought they were."

I pulled his hand away from his face and tipped his chin up for a kiss. Our lips had barely brushed when a sudden banging coming from outside interrupted us. Together, we left the office behind and raced outside to find the source of the unexpected noise.

Based on the racket, I expected to see an invading army, but instead all we discovered was Brody, hammering away at the frame of a new wall on Magnus's unfinished house.

"Um, Brody?" Magnus asked, approaching the construction zone with caution. "What are you doing?"

Brody stood on the top of a ladder and kept his eyes on his work. "Finishing your damn house."

Magnus stood at the bottom of the ladder. When Brody extended one hand toward him, he immediately grabbed the nail gun sitting on the workbench nearby and handed it over.

"Okay. Um, that's great, but why? Is this really the priority right now."

"It is," Brody grunted as he lined up the nail gun.

Apparently, he used hand nails to

temporarily set the frame of the wall in place, and then used the nail gun to properly secure everything. He nailed down one of the crossbeams, then wiggled it to make sure it was secure before moving onto the next. Before lining up the nail gun with the next beam, he cast a glance over at Magnus and me.

"If Casanova is going to be hanging around, then we're finishing your house as soon as possible, because I'm not spending one more night listening to you two."

My face burned so hot I was in danger of starting a wildfire. Next to me, Magnus wasn't much better.

Brody had heard us last night. I couldn't even remember everything we'd said or done, but I knew we hadn't been quiet.

Without another word, Magnus and I started helping Brody with the construction. I didn't know much about building houses, but I could hold things in place when directed, and hitting a nail with a hammer wasn't too hard to figure out.

After a couple hours of work, we managed to get one wall completely built, and a new frame started for a second wall. The foundation of the house had already been laid, and I could see the general shape that the house would take. It mostly seemed the same as Brody's house, except more of the rooms were on the ground floor with only the master suite on the small second floor.

"I prefer to keep my feet on the ground as much as possible," Magnus said with a shrug when I asked him about the layout. "My original plan was to have everything on one floor, but we were limited on the amount of foundational concrete we were able to get our hands on. Rather than wait, I decided to change the layout. Now, I like the idea of the main bedroom being up higher so I can look over my garden. It'll be a good view once I get the land and the greenhouse finished."

It was a lovely image. I could easily picture Magnus waking up and opening his windows to survey his land, making plans for all the greenery as if it were an army of plant-life in need of marching orders.

We took a break from our work for a late lunch, sitting amongst the results of our hard work. There weren't any chairs, so Magnus got comfortable on the bare foundation while Brody sat on an overturned crate. I managed to drag a pile of unused lumber closer to the foundation and turned the stack of wood into a bearable seat.

It wasn't the most comfortable lunch, but I wouldn't have changed anything about it. With sweat making my shirt stick to my back, Magnus laughing over a joke Brody had rhymed off, and the dogs sniffing around our feet for crumbs, I felt more at home than I had since the death of my grandparents.

The tranquility was interrupted by the sound of an approaching vehicle.

The approaching visitor could have been completely innocent, but with everything that had happened recently, all three of us were on edge. Brody was already reaching for his gun and Magnus had apparently attached a knife to his belt at some point during the day while I wasn't looking because he pulled the blade a few inches from its sheath.

I felt out of place as the only one who wasn't armed but tried to keep my cool as an unfamiliar truck finally rounded the bend and pulled into sight.

Whoever was in the truck didn't immediately step out after parking on the gravel patch. We waited in silence, staring at the truck like a standoff in an old western movie. Except no one was standing. Together, the three of us were the picture of nonchalance, relaxing together in the middle of our construction zone, but that couldn't have been further from the truth.

Eventually, we won the standoff, and the truck door opened.

Deputy Hillard jumped down from the driver's seat.

Magnus, Brody, and I were all instantly on our feet. Even the dogs stood to attention as Deputy Hillard approached the half-built house.

I looked down at his shoes. They were the same pair he'd worn before, but now the laces were black instead of white. I tried to tell myself that this meant nothing. He'd simply found better replacements in the days since I last saw him, but doubt still flickered in my mind.

Maybe I had been wrong. Maybe Deputy Hillard never tried to break into my shop, and I'd been blaming an innocent man all this time.

Deputy Hillard stopped when he was still a good distance away, eyeing the half-finished structure around us, which consisted mostly of freestanding walls and bare concrete floors.

"Looks like you've made some progress since we were here last."

The dogs growled at him, but they weren't as aggressive with the Deputy as they'd been with Carlton, choosing to stay back behind their masters.

Crossing his arms, Magnus leaned against one of the house's exposed support pillars, making sure to only apply weight to places he knew were reinforced.

"Well, my garden has been set back up after you guys tore up so much of it, so we decided to focus on a different project for now."

Deputy Hillard nodded along like this was just a casual conversation, but the hair on the back of my neck stood on end when his gaze shifted to focus on me.

"And Trent here just decided to help you out because he really likes vegetables?"

Magnus and I shared a look, each of us silently asking with our eyes what the other wanted to do. Just because we were comfortable being open with our relationship around Brody didn't mean we were ready to advertise it to the whole town.

Thankfully, Brody saved us from having to come up with a believable excuse by shouldering his way past me, so he stood at the front of our little group, right at the edge of the half-finished house.

"We're free to invite whoever we want onto our property, but you haven't been invited. So, if you don't mind me asking, what are you doing here?"

Deputy Hillard tried to keep staring at me, but Brody was a large man and hard to look past.

"I'm here on official business. We gave Mister Earhart permission to look at some evidence for us, but we haven't heard anything back since. I'm here to find out if you've made any progress."

Magnus also stepped up to stand in front of me, creating a nearly impenetrable wall between the Deputy and me.

I happily stayed right where I was.

"You could have just called rather than come all the way out here."

Deputy Hillard tried again to make eye contact with me, then sighed when he realized it was impossible. "I stopped by your place first, since it was near the station, but you weren't home. Your neighbors said you hadn't been home in a few days, so I got worried. One of them said they thought they'd seen you leave with Mister McGuire, so I figured I'd look here first."

"How… diligent." Brody turned to look at me over his shoulder, keeping himself angled so he never fully exposed his back to Deputy Hillard.

"Trent, you left the locket in my house. Why don't you go get it so you can show the Deputy what you found."

My feet carried me away from the scene and toward Brody's house without my conscious input.

Show the Deputy what I'd found?

Surely Brody didn't intend to reveal the secrets we'd found in the locket so easily.

But, what else could we do?

The locket was technically police property that I'd only been borrowing. If Deputy Hillard wanted it back, I had no reason to deny him.

The moment the door to the house closed behind me, I leaned my back against it and pulled the locket out of my pocket. I'd kept it with me this whole time, and could have handed it over immediately, but Brody had given me the perfect excuse to gather my wits and think.

I'd only been asked to restore the picture inside the locket, so that's all I needed to show Deputy Hillard. I could easily play dumb about the locket's hidden compartment.

Yet, a thought kept nagging at me.

Assuming I'd been right about Deputy Hillard's shoelaces, that meant he already knew about the mausoleum.

What if he already knew about the locket's secret compartment?

If he opened it up and found nothing, then he'd be suspicious.

Possibly even violent, depending on how much he cared about the secrets of the locket.

I had to put the items we'd found back in the secret compartment. We'd already taken pictures of the map, so that wouldn't be too great a loss, though I hated handing it over so easily.

It took me a few minutes to track down where we'd stored the map, and then figure out how to fold it up small enough to fit inside the locket's compartment.

As I was doing this, another idea occurred to me, and I made a quick pit stop to Brody's kitchen. Then, with the locket whole once again, I made my way back to the others.

Brody, Magnus, and Deputy Hillard were in the middle of a heated discussion when I returned.

"What do you mean you still don't know?" Magnus demanded.

The argument must have been going on for a while because Deputy Hillard looked even more on edge than when I left. "It's not easy to identify a body that is a hundred and twenty-five years old. It's not like we can just run a DNA test."

Magnus didn't look any more appeased

by this answer. "Well, is the body male or female. Surely you could at least tell that much."

"Male," Deputy Hillard spat out through clenched teeth. "And that's about all we know."

Male. So that ruled out one of the Milford sisters being the body in the coffin. Although, it did make Carlton's claim about his ancestor seem more credible. Perhaps Jacob Thornley really had been found.

Tossing his braided hair over his shoulder, Magnus let out a scoff and rolled his eyes. "Even I've watched enough crime shows to know how to identify if a body is male or female. Have the professional investigators done anything else, or is that the extent of your job?"

I'd seen Magnus fight before, so I knew how powerful his punches could be. Apparently, he could throw words with equal force. Each sound that came out of his mouth sounded like the opening of a fight, and Brody didn't seem inclined to stop him.

I quickly intervened before any actual fists started swinging.

"Here you are, Deputy." I held out the locket by its chain, letting it swing just under his nose. "I've cleaned up the picture inside as much as I could, though I have no idea who it's showing. If the body was a male, then I doubt the person in the picture was the victim."

Deputy Hillard snatched the locket from me so fast the chain left a red line against my palm.

I refused to show any sign of weakness and kept a smile on my face as I stepped back toward the structure of the half-finished house where Magnus and Brody were waiting.

Deputy Hillard turned the locket over in his hands. I expected him to leave now that he'd gotten what he'd come for, and for a moment it looked like that's exactly what he would do. He took a step in the direction of his truck, but then stopped and glanced back at us. A thought turned over in his head. I could see something moving behind his eyes but couldn't tell what direction his ideas pointed.

Then, to my surprise, he activated the latch hidden among the locket's carved petals and opened the secret compartment.

Magnus, Brody, and I all gaped at him. The fact that he already knew about the locket's secrets came as no shock, but for him to open it right in front of us was...

I couldn't even begin to imagine what it meant.

From the secret compartment, he pulled out the folded paper, unwrapping it to reveal the map and the coffee beans stored inside.

He didn't even try to pretend to be shocked. If anything, he looked smug as he tipped the contents of the locket up at us, like a salute, then turned around and finally left.

No one said a word until the Deputy's car disappeared between the trees.

"That fucking bastard," Magnus growled.

I rubbed the palm of my hand, soothing the sting there now that I felt safe enough to show signs of pain. "What was that about? Why did he just open it in front of us?"

Brody was as still as a statue, arms crossed, and feet planted wide like he was still ready to charge into a fight at any moment.

"He was testing us. He wanted to see our reaction to try and catch us in a lie."

Noticing the wound on my palm, Magnus grabbed my hand and started rubbing the red skin to soothe the sting.

"Or he was just gloating. Either showing off the secret we failed to find, or the fact that we had to hand it over in the end. He's right, too. We have pictures of the map, but we never figured out what was special about the coffee beans. I wish I could have examined them some more. Figure out why someone would go to such lengths to hide them"

"You might still have that chance." I grinned at him, and with the hand not currently held captive by Magnus, I pulled several coffee beans out of my pocket. "I stole a few beans from your kitchen and swapped them out. It's a good thing you've got that fancy coffee machine and don't just use the instant stuff."

Magnus and Brody both looked at the beans cupped in my palm in shock before Magnus grabbed me by both shoulders.

"You beautiful trickster. I think I'm in love."

I had no time to respond to his compliment—and his loaded use of the word *love*—before he pulled me into a kiss.

Most of my brain turned to useless jelly when Magnus wrapped his arms around me, but a small fraction of my mind remained clear enough to notice Brody grabbing the coffee beans from my hand before I dropped them.

"I'll go store these somewhere safe and, uh... give you two some space."

His boots echoed across the half-built foundation as he left, and then Magnus and I were blessedly alone.

He pushed me up against one of the walls we'd just built, pinning my wrists to the wood as his tongue plundered my mouth. I couldn't resist, nor did I want to, and kissed back with equal fervor.

Time stood still and the earth stopped spinning as we stood there in the skeleton of what would someday be Magnus's home.

At least, that's what it felt like. In reality, it was probably only a few minutes before we broke apart, each out of breath and panting.

"Fuck," Magnus groaned as he leaned his forehead against mine. "I really want you right now, but..."

"But it'd be awkward to make Brody listen to us again," I finished for him.

"Yeah." With a deep sigh Magnus stood up and looked at the structure around us. "Now I wish I'd focused on getting my house built sooner. Then we'd have somewhere private."

I wrapped my arms around his shoulders, not ready to be fully parted from him yet. "Don't worry about it. There's no rush. Like I said, I'm not going anywhere."

Even with his pupils still blown wide with lust, Magnus's gaze drifted to where Deputy Hillard had been standing just a few minutes ago.

"We may have to go somewhere. We're not going to figure out what's going on just hanging around here. I'm glad you managed to hang onto the coffee beans, but I don't know what to do next."

Leaning against him so my mouth was right next to his ear, I kept my voice to a soft whisper. "You know, I had a thought about that."

Magnus wrapped his arm around my waist and slipped it into my back pocket where he could easily grab my ass.

"Yeah? Well, lay it on me. I'm all ears."

"My grandparents collected a lot of stuff. One of the things they collected was old newspapers. I've still got most of them, some of them dating all the way back to the founding of Emberwood. If Jacob Thornley's disappearance was noteworthy enough to make the local news, then there might be something written about it in one of those newspapers."

Magnus pulled back just enough to look me in the eye. "That sounds like a fantastic idea. I'll tell Brody where we're going, and we'll head over to your shop."

"Great," I said, already stepping away from him toward his car. "The newspapers are well organized by date, so hopefully, it won't take too long."

I didn't get more than a step away before the arm around my waist pulled me back, and Magnus squeezed my ass harder.

"We might be gone longer than you think," he said while kissing my neck.

His lips trailed all the way from my shoulder to my jaw and stopped right at the sensitive spot behind my ear, making me shiver.

"Your apartment has a bed, right?"

CHAPTER NINE

Magnus

WE FORGOT ALL about the newspapers even before we reached Trent's shop. While I was driving us into town, he started stroking his hand along my thigh, and all I could think about was the privacy available in the apartment above the shop.

I had barely stopped my truck in the parking space on the street before we were hurrying out and into the shop. We were delayed a moment as Trent deactivated the security system, which he'd kept extra locked down while he was gone. It only took a minute, but that extra delay felt like it lasted hours as my blood burned under my skin.

Luckily, it was a quiet town. Even under the sun of midmorning, there weren't many people out on the street to see me bouncing on the balls of my feet like an impatient child.

Finally, we were inside the shop with the front door closed behind us. I couldn't wait to get upstairs to the apartment, where a bed awaited us. Instead, I pushed Trent up against the front desk where he kept the ancient cash register. The bell on the solid iron and brass machine clanged when our combined weight slid the entire desk a few inches across the floor, but I paid it no mind as my mouth crashed against Trent's in a heated kiss.

Last night, he'd been the one to take charge, and I'd enjoyed the opportunity to be spoiled for once. However, now I intended to return the favor. I crowded Trent against the desk, hands planted to either side of his hips on the flat surface to cage him in as I nipped at his lips and pushed my tongue forcefully into his mouth.

Trent was a willing captive, tangling his hands in my hair and pulling me closer.

We leaned farther across the desk, putting a lot of faith in the craftsmanship of the old furniture as Trent's feet left the floor. The desk had been carved from a sturdy piece of oak, and age and care had only strengthened the wood over time. It didn't even groan as it supported all of Trent's weight and most of mine, and we were free to lose ourselves in each other without fear.

This was a mistake. We should have probably kept our guard up. Then we wouldn't have been surprised by the sound of the front door opening.

"Hey, Trent. You're finally back. Where'd you disapea—woah!"

I jumped away from Trent so fast I nearly tripped over the matching chair sitting near the desk.

Trent took an extra second to realize what had happened, lying half sprawled across the wooden surface, but when he did, he also jumped to his feet with a flaming blush on his face.

An unfamiliar woman stood in the doorway to the shop, staring at us with a surprised yet wary expression.

"Trent? Uh, who's this?"

Even if she hadn't addressed Trent so casually, I would have immediately known they were related. They looked too similar for them to not share blood.

Same dark hair.

Same strong nose and expressive brows.

She even had the same muscular build

as him, though her frame came with added feminine curves.

Trent nervously smoothed down his shirt, as if getting rid of the wrinkles there would wipe away the evidence of what we'd just been doing.

"Uh, Lea. Hi. This is Magnus." He couldn't look at either of us as he gestured between us with a halfhearted introduction. "Magnus, this is Lea. My sister."

Lea and I regarded each other coolly, clearly not knowing what to do with this new person that had unexpected entered our lives. Eventually, we both took a step forward and shook hands like we were participating in the world's most awkward business meeting.

"Magnus McGuire," I introduced myself, making sure to look her in the eye the whole time. "I moved into Old Milford's place a few months ago."

Her grip was strong, and thick calluses

lined her palm. "Oh, right. I heard someone was trying to turn that barren piece of land into an eco-friendly farm or something. I wasn't expecting the person behind it to be so..."

She trailed off, eyeing me up and down in a way that wasn't flattering, but wasn't outright insulting either. It felt more a sniper staring down the scope of their gun, still trying to decide where or not to pull the trigger.

With Brody and Creed as friends, I had plenty of experience with this kind of look and knew better than to poke a dog that was still lying down.

"So," she finally said when she finished her initial observation of me. "Magnus. What brings you here? Last I checked, antiques had little to do with farming."

"Lea," Trent hissed under his breath.

"What?" she rounded on her brother, and for the first time I could see that the leather jacket she wore was actually a biker jacket. "You can't expect me to not ask any questions. I didn't even know you were seeing anyone and then I walk in to find you spreading your legs in the front room of Nana and Papa's shop."

She stormed up to Trent, easily intimidating him despite her shorter height. A heavy scowl pulled at her brow, and for a moment, I feared I would have to break up a fight, especially when Trent shied away from her.

However, her frown quickly changed into a smile as she punched Trent hard in the arm.

"Good for you, you big ol' slut. I thought I was going to have to drag you onto a date by your nose hairs one day, but here you are getting some all on your own."

Trent laughed sheepishly under his breath, hunching his shoulders and making himself seem about two feet shorter.

"Yeah, well, it's kind of a new thing. We're still..." His gaze flickered over toward me too quick for me to school my reaction into something neutral, so I had no idea what kind of expression I was making in that moment. "We're still figuring it out."

Lea punched Trent in the arm again, lighter this time. "Obviously, I have to hear all the details. Get me a drink, dork. It was a six-hour ride to get here, and I'm parched."

Trent bobbed his head in immediate agreement and headed toward the shop's back room to follow her order.

As he left, she called after him. "And don't get that cheap stuff I know you like drinking. Get me the good stuff Papa kept hidden in the old chest that he thought was a secret."

As soon as Trent was out of sight, her smile disappeared and her eyes locked onto me.

"I know Trent said you're still figuring it out, but I'm required to tell you that if you hurt him, I've got about a dozen friends willing to help me hide a body."

Her attitude, from her direct words down to the very way she stood, reminded me so much of other soldiers I'd served with that I couldn't help but laugh. Even the way part of her hair was buzzed reminded me of the military.

"Your friends sound a lot like my friends. I'm not sure if that means we should introduce them or keep them as far apart from each other as possible."

With the customary intimidations out of the way, Lea and I fell into a much easier conversation. The shop didn't have a lot of places to sit. Even the back room could only fit two people comfortably. So, instead, we created a little sitting area out of a few pieces of antique furniture that was piled along the back wall.

It turned out that Lea was short for

Leanira. It was an unusual name, but very pretty. When she was younger, she'd gone by her full name, but after getting sick of constantly have to explain how pronounce it, she shortened it to Lea.

Just as Trent returned, placing a glass of rich and very expensive alcohol on the table in front of her, I noticed the lettering on the back of her jacket. At first, I hadn't thought much about the insignia other than the fact that I clearly marked her as a member of a biker gang, but when I got a closer look I realized that I didn't recognize the abbreviation.

"Oh, this?" she said when I asked about the letters on her jacket which spelled out B.A.C.A. "I'm not surprised you don't recognize it. Not many people do. It stands for Bikers Against Child Abuse. We help protect kids going through difficult court cases. A lot of them must appear in courtrooms where they are forced to face their abusers directly in order to testify. It's traumatic for them, especially for people so young, but showing up to court with an entourage of a bunch of scary looking bikers as their personal bodyguards can be very empowering."

As she spoke of her work, a large grin spread across her face, equal parts joyful and menacing.

"Basically, we use the scary reputation that biker gangs have to our advantage."

She was right. I'd never heard of such a thing, but learning about it now, I wished I'd known sooner.

"We've been real busy lately. A big pedophile ring was busted a while ago, so there have been a lot of trials. My gang has been traveling around the country, trying to help with as many as possible. I've only just now gotten enough of a break to come back home for a while." Her expression had turned serious when talking about her work, but it shifted back into a sly grin when he looked at me.

"I have to say, seeing my brother getting pinned to his desk wasn't the sight I expected to greet me the minute I came back home."

"Lea," Trent whined again, drawing out the sound of her name into an entire sentence.

She responded by pinching the skin on his leg until he flinched.

"I'm just teasing. Don't take it so seriously. It's about time you got a boyfriend so I can stop worrying about you."

Rubbing at the spot where she pinched him, Trent mumbled under his breath.

"We're not really... we haven't... discussed it that much."

Although I hadn't known Trent that long, I thought I had a pretty good understanding of him. That idea was thrown right out the window when I realized I wasn't sure what he was talking about, while Lea clearly understood what his disjointed sentences mean.

"Oh, I see." She nodded before gesturing between the two of us with her drink. "So, this is just, like, a casual thing? Friends with benefits. I get it."

"No," I immediately disagreed. "We're not... we're not that."

I wasn't sure how to label our relationship. We hadn't discussed labels, but I hated the possibility that Trent thought I was only interested in sex.

I looked over at him to see the other man with his mouth hanging open, like he'd been about to talk but was interrupted before he could make a sound.

Lea, meanwhile, leaned back in her chair with a satisfied smile, and I knew I'd walked right into her trap.

"Ah, so you are dating."

"Lea," Trent said again, this time hissing her name like he wanted to hit her with it.

Who knew a single word could be said in so many different ways.

Lea took one look at the blush on Trent's face and burst out laughing. "Oh, you dork. Stop getting so embarrassed. You're forty-two, not a teenager with his first crush. You should be able to talk about relationship stuff without getting so flustered."

"I can talk about it," Trent immediately protested, though his voice lacked its usual conviction. "We've just, had a lot of things to worry about instead."

This, of course, lead to an explanation of the last few days, including the body that had been dug up on my property, the locket, the mausoleum, and the different people who had either directly or indirectly threatened us.

"That's actually why we're here," Trent said when we finished explaining everything. "I've still got Grandpa's collection of old newspapers. I was hoping we might find something about Jacob Thornley's murder."

In an eerily similar gesture, Trent and Lea both looked over at a large metal cabinet where I assumed the old newspaper collection was stored.

"Without a more specific date, that's a lot of papers to go through. I don't suppose you'd want some help with that?"

Trent and I both immediately agreed to her offer, and together the three of us started the arduous task of sorting through all the old newspapers.

The metal cabinet was bigger in the inside than it seemed, practically its own little room, and significant portion of that space was dedicated to stacks and stacks of newspapers. Their age was obvious in the amount of yellowing the newsprint paper had undergone over time, and with how meticulously they had been sorted, they created a gradient from pristine white on one end to almost brown on the other.

We ignored the newer papers, and Trent pulled out a stack from the older end. The paper was so brittle it reminded me of dried autumn leaves, and I was almost afraid to touch it as Trent spread it over a table.

Emberwood still had the same newspaper today as it did over a century ago. The very straightforwardly named *The Weekly Reporter* could still be found regularly sitting on doorsteps and mailboxes waiting to be read. The only difference between modern newspapers and the older ones was the font of the lettering. Back then, each newspaper had still been manually typeset and printed by hand, so the letters weren't quite as clean or perfectly aligned as a computer could do now. To make up for it, however, there was more character and extra elements added to the font, turning each printing into its own little work of art.

Manually printing newspapers one by one was a lot of work. If people back then were going to go through all the effort, then they probably wanted to make sure the product they were making was worth that effort.

Trent picked up one for himself then handed other ones to Lea and me. "Don't bother reading the whole thing. Just pay attention to headlines. Once you've finished looking through one, hand it back to me so I can keep everything organized."

I picked up the newspaper that he'd handed to me, while at the same time Lea nudged me with her elbow.

"He's so obsessive about everything in this shop. I swear, I don't think he's moved anything from where it was when our grandparents ran the place.

Although she was making fun of her brother, she also had a smile on her face and clearly didn't mean anything bad by the comment.

I found the whole thing cute. Looking around the shop, I could easily picture Trent when he was a young child helping his grandparents manage the place. When he was really little, he was probably more hindrance than help, but over the years, he'd have gotten better until he could run the shop without a second thought.

Lea tapped me with her elbow again, looking pointedly at the newspaper I was supposed to be searching through. There was an unusually soft smile on her face.

She knew exactly what I'd just been picturing.

Headlines in *The Weekly Reporter* were surprisingly interesting. Small town life didn't offer much exciting news, but the writers of the newspaper managed to make it sound much more interesting with headlines like *Man Killed By His Own Sheep* and *Raining Frogs Terrorize Local*

Citizens. In the first one, a farmer had chocked while eating a lamb chop which came from his own flock, and the second one had been a prank where some boys collected a bunch of frogs and dropped them on people from a third story window.

Trent had told us not to bother reading the articles, but I couldn't help scanning through the contents. Each article was a fascinating little snippet into the lives of people who lived a hundred and twenty-five years ago.

It turned out, their lives weren't so different from ours. Any of these headlines could have easily appeared on a modern newspaper.

Even with three people working together, there was still a lot to go through. We didn't have anything to narrow down a time frame, other than the estimated age of the locket. So, we ended up starting all the way back around the time of the fire that gave the town of Emberwood its name and working our way forward through time. A lot of property had been lost in the fire, including newspapers, so there wasn't much from before this time. If the murder had happened before the fire, then we'd likely find nothing about it, so we started immediately after the fire and hoped we'd get lucky.

One saving grace was the fact that *The Weekly Reporter*, as evidenced by its name, was a weekly publication rather than a daily one. So, there were only fifty-two newspapers per year. I estimated that we'd searched through about five years' worth of newspapers when we finally found something noteworthy.

"Look at this," Trent said as he spread a newspaper flat over the table.

The date at the top said January 15, 1907.

"Did you find something about Jacob

Thornley?" I asked as I angled by body to get a better look at the headline.

"No, but the headline mentions a conflict between the Thornley family and the Milford family."

It was actually one of the tamer headlines, getting straight to the point without much embellishment. *Blood Boils Between Milford and Thornley.* Even after reading the article, we still weren't entirely sure what the conflict had been about, other than it involved a land dispute regarding the town's mill.

"Oh, right, Milford," I said as I realized the connection out loud. "That name probably means they have something to do with the old mill."

An image of the map that we'd found in the locket sprung to mind. The path marked on the map lead to the hidden mausoleum, but it started at the remains of the old mill. I hadn't thought anything of it at the time other than the fact that the mill was a useful landmark, but perhaps there was a reason the map had used this as its starting point.

"That old mill was the first thing ever built on this land," Trent explained as he read through the article again. "The rest of the town grew up around it. The Milford family built it, hence their name, and that's why they are credited as the town's founders."

It was easy to forget that Trent had grown up in this town, unlike Brody and I, who had only moved in a few months ago. To him, the history of Emberwood was probably as common as grass and not worth a second thought.

I made a mental note to myself as a reminder to pick his brain later about the history of Emberwood. There could be a lot of useful information hidden in plain sight that no one thought about simply because it was so well known.

Lea slid the newspaper closer to

herself to also give it a second look. "That could explain why Rose Milford killed Jacob Thornley. That mill would have been one of the most important pieces of land back then. But it still doesn't tell us anything about the murder, or why the Thornley family would still be holding a grudge about it all this time."

There were no more headlines about either the Milford or the Thornley family until about six months later, when the article we were looking for finally appeared. Like the earlier article about the land dispute, this one was also written in a very straightforward manner and was given far less space within the newspaper than such an event would typically earn. It wasn't even on the front page, but randomly stuffed between two articles about crop rotations and the completion of a new city hall building.

There was also barely any mention of Rose Milford or anyone from the Milford family. The way the article was worded in a way so that anyone reading it couldn't even be certain that the man in question was dead. He was simply referred to as "gone" and was given a few generic condolences about being missed.

It was the most impersonal report of a possible murder that I'd ever seen.

"This is the only part that's any help," Lea said as she indicated a few sentences near the bottom of the article. "Apparently a few weeks earlier Jacob Thornley had tried breaking into Rose Milford's house. That might be why the Thornley family assumed she killed him, but the article doesn't seem to treat it like a motive for murder. If anything, it just seems to treat his death as inevitable."

Trent carefully took the old paper from her and read the article more carefully for himself, but the words remained the same and he found nothing more useful.

"You're right, this doesn't tell us much.

But it does at least confirm that what Carlton Thornley said is possible. And it gives us a date to work with. Considering this all happened around the same time that locket was made, I still suspect that the two things are connected."

He set the newspaper aside and started organizing the other ones back into their carefully organized stacks.

I offered to help, but Trent shoed me away, claiming that I wouldn't understand his grandfather's organization system. I could have argued that I understood how to order things by date just fine, but I stayed quiet. It wasn't meant as an insult to me, but rather an excuse for Trent to handle the objects of the shop on his own.

To me *Memory Lane* was just a shop, but I was starting to realize that it was a part of Trent's identity, and everything inside it had to be arranged just so.

My observation was validated by the

fact that Lea didn't even offer to help her brother. She stayed seated right where she was, eyes slightly glazed as she was lost in her own thoughts.

I enjoyed myself watching Trent shuffling around the shop, carefully navigating aisles that weren't built for a man his size without bumping into a single thing. It was impressive, honestly, and watching him move with such delicacy was strangely attractive.

"Something's bugging me," Lea spoke up from just a foot away.

I quickly turned my attention to her, trying to hide my thoughts and pretend that I hadn't just been ogling her brother.

"There's a lot of things bugging me about this case. Most importantly, the body I found on my land that's still unidentified."

"Yeah," she agreed. "It sucks that we couldn't confirm whether the body you found is actually Jacob Thornley or not, but this is about something else. The three Milford sisters. Rose, Lisianthus, and Poppy. Something about the combination of those three flowers seems familiar, but I can't remember why."

I tried to recall any time I'd seen those three flowers together before, but nothing came to mind and I shook my head. "They're all common garden flowers, though they grow in different levels of light. Could you have seen them together in someone's garden?"

"No, it's not that." She tapped her fingers together in a senseless rhythm. The lack of a discernable pattern set my teeth on edge, and I went back to watching Trent put away the last of the newspapers.

If I had a choice, any view with him in it was better than one without.

This time there was no hiding the direction of my thoughts, and Lea gave me a knowing smile.

"Well, I think that's enough sleuthing for one day. My brain hurts from all that reading, so I'll be hitting a few bars on my way home. I assume the two of you aren't interested in coming."

Neither Trent nor I had time to answer before Lea was grabbing her leather jacket off the back of her chair and swinging it over her shoulders.

"Great. Tell me if you find out anything else, and I'll let you know if I remember where I've seen those three flowers before. All right? All right. Bye."

And just like that, as quickly as she'd arrived, she was gone.

"Well," I said after a moment staring after her in shock. "Your sister's a real whirlwind, isn't she."

Trent's hand landed on my shoulder. "Yeah. She's always had a habit of blowing in when it suits her, then blowing right back out again. We might see her later. We might not. Who knows."

His leg swung over me, and before I knew what was happening, he was sitting in my lap.

"But you don't really want to waste time talking about my sister, right. Now that she's gone, we can pick up where we left off."

Cupping my face on either side, he pulled me into a kiss. It was like we hadn't been interrupted at all. The heat inside me, which had been smothered the moment Lea walked through the door, instantly burst to life again, burning me from the inside out.

I grabbed him without thought or care, simply digging my fingers into whatever flesh they could find. His shirt was quickly lost to the floor, and mine wasn't far behind when we were interrupted by an ominous cracking sound.

I pulled away from the kiss.

"Wha—"

The question never fully left my lips.

Before I could finish forming a single word, the world suddenly shifted as the chair beneath us broke and we were both sent tumbling to the floor.

All the air was knocked from my lungs as Trent's elbow planted heavily in my solar plexus, and his leg smacked heavily against the nearby table. Luckily, there was a plush rug lining the floor, just as old but well maintained as everything else in the shop, or I would have been at risk of a concussion when my head hit the floor.

We lay tangled together there on the floor for a few silent moments trying to process what had happened.

Out of the corner of my eye, I saw the remains of the chair I'd just been sitting in. One leg had completely snapped off and another was hanging on only by a few splinters. It had once been a solidly built piece of furniture but supporting both Trent and I had been too much to ask for something made of such old wood.

"I hope that wasn't expensive," I said as I nodded at the chair.

Trent stared down at me with his eyes so wide I could nearly see the whites all the way around his dark irises. His breathing came faster, and a flush stained his cheeks.

Was he mad?

I was only joking at first, but maybe the chair actually had been expensive.

In my mind, I started tallying up the funds available in my bank account, hoping I'd be able to afford the antique if it needed to be replaced.

I didn't even notice that Trent started laughing until the feeling of his stomach jerking against mine alerted me.

"Don't worry," Trent managed to gasp out between his laughter. "It wasn't an antique. Just an old chair."

His laughter kicked up even stronger, and he buried his face against my shoulder.

His breath tickled my neck, and I shifted my legs under his weight to try and hide my reaction to his body pressed so close to mine.

I did not want to explain why I was getting an erection while being laughed at.

"It's not that funny."

Trent's laughter slowed, but there was still a smile on his face when he finally looked up, though he was still lying half on top of me.

"I'm not laughing at you. I promise. It's just... First Brody. Then my sister. Now this. It feels like the universe is trying to tell us something."

"Trying to make me die of blue balls. That's what it's trying to do."

This time, Trent's laughter was a mere puff of air. More smirk than actual laughter as he trailed his hand down my side toward the clasp of my pants.

MAGNUS

"I can do something about that."

I was so eager for any attention from him, that he managed to get my pants halfway down my thighs before I realized this wasn't what I'd wanted.

Each time we'd had sex or been intimate before, Trent had always been the one to take charge. It was a refreshing difference to how things usually worked, but that didn't mean I wanted to be on the receiving end every time.

There was just as much pleasure to found in giving.

Pushing on Trent's shoulders, I flipped him over so he was lying flat on his back on the floor.

"Not this time. You've had me at your mercy before. Now, it's my turn."

My own half-removed pants were only getting in the way, so I removed them completely before turning my attention to the belt keeping Trent's pants in place. I was too eager to take the time stripping him completely naked, and only pulled his pants and underwear down far enough for his arousal to spring free.

He was just as hard as I was. Just as eager. It was a heady sensation, knowing my partner was eager for me, and my mouth watered with anticipation.

As I myself between his legs, the rug beneath us scratched against my bare stomach as I leaned forward to run my tongue up his cock from root to tip. I couldn't see Trent's expression from my position, but I heard him moan and felt him shift as his head tipped back and his spine arched.

My own cock throbbed between my legs. The sound of his moans mixed with the taste of him on my tongue was better than any aphrodisiac.

Greedy for more, I swallowed him whole, taking as much of his cock into my mouth as I could until it hit the back of my throat. I didn't have enough experience to control my gag reflex, so that was as far as I could go, but Trent didn't seem to mind that I couldn't swallow him completely. His whole body writhed against the floor and he buried his hands in my hair to guide my motions toward the spots that felt best as I sucked and licked at his arousal.

I let him guide me, following his silent commands like a puppet being yanked around by my strings. Even when I tried to take charge, I ended up following his lead, but I was too lost in my own pleasure to care.

As I bobbed my head up and down over him, I allowed my own hand to travel down to grip my weeping, desperate cock. I stroked myself at the same pace as I pleasured him, always in tandem so we were driven toward the height of our pleasure at the same pace.

Something twisted tight in my gut just before my orgasm hit me hard. Electricity danced under my skin and lightning danced behind my eyes like my own personal fireworks. I moaned as I spilled over my own hand, staining the carpet beneath us.

Trent gasped as the sounds of my pleasure vibrated around his cock, and his back arched violently. He slipped partially out of my mouth, so when he came, he not only coated my tongue but also my neck and chest with his release.

The milky white liquid dripped down my chest, causing hair and skin to stick together in a way that was going to be a pain to wash out.

However, that was future me's problem. The me of right now was content to simply lie on the floor with my head pillowed on Trent's thigh as we both caught our breath, and completely ignore the mess that we'd made of ourselves.

One of Trent's hands idly stroked my hair, finger combing out the tangles that he'd put there.

"I was planning on having you in a proper bed." He smiled down at me, tired but satisfied. "You have a bad habit of derailing my plans."

I didn't need a bed when his thigh made such an excellent pillow. It was just the right combination of soft and firm. I could have lain there all day and didn't even bother to raise my head as I grinned up at him.

"I gotta keep things interesting. Otherwise, you might get bored of me."

With an exhausted groan, Trent managed to sit up just enough to bring us closer together.

"That's never gonna happen."

He bent himself into an awkward position with the obvious intent to kiss me. So, although I was perfectly happy where I was, I raised up onto my elbow to meet him halfway.

If he didn't care about the taste of

himself on my tongue, then I wasn't going to turn him down.

Our hands had barely brushed when the sound of a phone ringing interrupted us. We paused, close enough to breathe each other's air, as we both silently debated what to do.

My first instinct was to ignore the phone. Nothing could be more important than the warmth of Trent's lips pressed against mine.

Then I recognized the ringtone.

Immediately jumping into action, I grabbed up my pants, but found the pockets empty. When the chair had collapsed, my phone must have been knocked from my pocket. It was nowhere in the immediate area, so I searched under the nearby furniture and antiques. Following the sound of the ringtone, I eventually found the lost device hiding under a bookshelf, and managed to press the answer button just before the it switched over to voicemail.

"Creed," I gasped into the phone. "What is it? What's wrong?"

Creed, the third member of our little off-grid homestead operation, was still serving out the final months of his service. Getting a phone call to us from overseas was often difficult, so for him to be calling me unexpectedly must mean it was something important.

"Mag," his familiar gruff voice greeted me. "I heard about... Why the hell are you naked?"

I looked down at the phone, then at myself. In my rush to catch the call, I'd hit the answer button without properly looking at the screen. If I had, I would have realized it was a video call and not just a regular phone call. Creed's face stared up at me from the screen, his usually stoic expression slowly shifting to astonishment as he got a good look at me.

All of me.

"Fuck!"

I practically flung the phone away as I scrambled for my clothes.

In the background, I could hear Trent laughing again, and this time it was definitely at me.

CHAPTER TEN

Trent

MAGNUS PROBABLY BROKE some sort of world record with how fast he got dressed after accidentally answering his friend's video call. I'd barely blinked before suddenly finding his pants and shirt back in place, though very clearly disheveled.

Even dressed, there was still no denying what we'd just been doing.

Safely out of the phone camera's line of sight, I got dressed at a more leisurely pace. I positioned myself so I would remain out of view, while still being able to see the phone screen.

Magnus had told me about Creed before, and the man on the screen matched the description, yet was still nothing like I'd imagined.

Despite their size and abilities, Brody and Magnus still had an air of softness about them. In Brody's case, his teddy bear appearance was so convincing that it was a shock every time he displayed an aptitude for violence. Magnus was a little more intimidating, especially since my first glimpse of him was during a cage fight. Yet there was an earnestness to his expression that made his strength seem more protective than threatening.

Creed lacked any hint of softness. He had the same bulky build as Magnus and Brody, but on him such size only made him look stronger.

Like a bull that wasn't afraid to throw around its weight, or a wrecking ball that would easily bash right through a brick wall.

The man's gaze was sharp, and for a moment, it almost felt like he could see me even though I was nowhere near the camera. A jagged scar ran down from his temple, coming precariously close to his eye. I shuddered at the thought of what must have happened to the person who gave him such a wound.

The only thing that kept him from looking truly terrifying was the slight softness of his mouth when he looked at Magnus. It wasn't a full smile, but it was still a clearly affectionate expression.

This was one of the two people that Magnus valued most. For Magnus to care about him so much, then there must be a good guy hidden under such an intimidating appearance.

With my clothes mostly in place, I felt comfortable enough to sneak a little closer. Not enough to put myself in view of the camera, but enough to hear what Magnus and Creed were talking about.

"Of course I'm worried," Creed was saying. I couldn't see most of his body, but he was making some sort of angry gesture. "You find a dead body on the property, and now you're getting harassed by law enforcement, why wouldn't I be worried."

"It's fine," Magnus tried to insist while simultaneously continuing to fix his messy clothes one handed.

In response, Creed just gave him a disbelieving look. "Brody shot a guy."

"Well..." Magnus sucked air through his teeth as he cringed over his own words. "He shot *at* a guy. It was just a warning shot when the guy tried to sneak onto our property. Really. It's all fine. Don't worry about us. The only thing you should be focusing on is finishing out your service."

Since Creed looked like such a serious

person, I wasn't prepared for the way his face changed when he smiled. It wasn't a full smile, just a teasing smirk, but it practically made him look like a whole different person.

With this new view of Creed, it wasn't so surprising that he was friends with Magnus and Brody.

"Shut up, Mag." Even the low-quality speaker on Magnus's phone couldn't hide the fond mockery that laced though his voice. "Brody gave me a basic summary of the situation. He said you were looking into an old murder to try and identify the body that you found since the police are dragging their feet. Any luck?"

Magnus gave a very basic explanation of what we'd found in the old newspapers, leaving out any mention of my sister or me. Based on his recounting of events, it seemed like the newspapers spawned out of nowhere and Magnus searched through everything himself.

If it were anyone else, I would have assumed Magnus was trying to take credit for all the work, but that didn't fit his character. He'd never seemed to care about credit or stealing the spotlight before.

While he talked, Magnus's gaze drifted toward me several times before he quickly looked away and focused back on his phone screen.

A new, unpleasant thought occurred to me. Magnus was clearly out to Brody, but maybe the same wasn't true when it came to Creed.

Was he avoiding talking about me to Creed because his friend wouldn't accept our relationship?

If that was true, there would be no future for us. Magnus was in the process of building a home with his friends. It was obvious how much he cared about them. If it came down to a choice between them or me, it's obvious who would win.

MAGNUS

When Magnus finished his explanation, Creed thought in silence for a moment. His dark, heavy brows furrowed until they nearly touched in the middle and the soft smile completely disappeared from his face.

In the blink of an eye, the man returned to an intimidating figure.

After only a moment, he seemed to come to a decision and looked at Magnus with certainty in his eyes. Whatever he was about to say would decide what Magnus and I did next.

"You should go back to the mausoleum."

I wanted to ask for clarification. We'd already been to the mausoleum, and while the discovery of the hidden graves was interesting, it didn't help our situation now. However, I wasn't willing to put myself in Creed's line of sight and stayed silent far away from the screen on the phone.

Luckily, Magnus had the same questions as me and wasn't so hesitant about speaking up.

"Why? We've already been there. Do you think we missed something?"

The image on the phone screen showed just enough to reveal that Creed's hand was moving.

Was he writing something down?

He did seem to be holding a pencil.

No. The movement wasn't right. He was drawing. He barely looked at the page, and his hand seemed to move on instinct. Whatever he was drawing, it wasn't a part of the actual conversation.

"You've been to the mausoleum," Creed agreed. "But I'm more curious about the map that led you there. You found it in Rose Milford's locket, right?"

Magnus agreed, but based on the confused look on his face, I could tell that even he didn't know where Creed was going with this.

MAGNUS

At least I wasn't the only one confused.

Creed stopped drawing and he placed the pencil down out of sight. "Why would someone keep a map to their own grave inside their locket? The location must have had some significance even before she died. There were three sisters, so it could be something as simple as one of the sisters dying before Rose and the map marked the location of her sister's grave, but my instincts say there's something else to it."

That made sense, and I felt a bit foolish that I hadn't thought of it sooner. I took a step closer without thinking, nearly coming into the camera's view, but managed to stop myself just in time.

Luckily, Creed still hadn't noticed my presence.

"It's not just about the mausoleum," he said, going back to his idle sketching without ever looking at his hand. "The map had a very specific path drawn on it, starting from the old mill, which the Milford family also owned at the time, and leading to the mausoleum. When you made the trip out there, you started from our property, so you approached in from a different direction."

Understanding lit up Magnus's face.

"You think there's something significant about the specific path to get to the mausoleum."

In an unexpected gesture of indifference, Creed merely shrugged.

"Without being there myself, it's hard to say for certain, but that's what my instincts are saying."

When Magnus laughed, the air mostly passed through his nose, so it sounded more exasperated than humorous. "I know better than to ignore your instincts. All right. We'll head up to the mausoleum again as soon as we can. Luckily, we took a picture of the map, so we can still follow it."

MAGNUS

With a few final farewells and promises
to keep Creed updated on what happened,
Magnus eventually ended the video call
with a sigh.

As soon as the screen went dark, he
turned to me.

"Sorry about that. I wasn't trying to
cut you out of the conversation. It's
just..."

Grasping his hand in both of mine, I
took the phone from his grip and set it
aside so it was no longer between us.

"Does Creed not know that you're
gay?"

At first, Magnus immediately shook his
head, but then the gesture changed into
an uncertain side to side motion like he
couldn't decide whether to say yes or no.

"It's not that. He knows about me, and
about Brody, too, but Creed's still got one
foot in the closet. Logically, he knows that
he's gay, too. We all know. But he hasn't
fully accepted it yet and can get squirrelly

whenever something reminds him about it."

"I understand." I wrapped my arms around his shoulders to pull him closer, and he easily stepped into my embrace. "I was worried that you were embarrassed about me, but I can see why you wouldn't want to have that conversation over the phone. Although..." I pulled back just enough to look directly into his eyes. "I hope that you don't plan to keep our relationship from him forever. You've said that the plan is for Creed to eventually join you and Brody on your property. When that happens, you won't be able to get away with just not telling him anything, and I refuse to be anyone's secret. I lived in the closet long enough when I was young, and I don't plan on going back in."

Although there were only a few inches of space between us, that was apparently too much for Magnus. He wrapped his arms tight around me and pulled me close until the entire line of our bodies pressed together.

"I'm not going to keep you a secret. I just need to find the right time to tell Creed about it. Besides, he probably already suspects something. He's a very observant person, and the state I answered the phone in was... well, not subtle."

The memory of Magnus's panicked face when he realized he'd answered a video call immediately had me laughing again.

"Yes. I wished I'd been recording that moment. You should have seen your reaction. It was so over the top, like something out of a cartoon."

Magnus pinched my side, making me yelp in surprise.

"Stop laughing," he grumbled. "It wasn't funny. I've never been so embarrassed."

He tried to pinch me again, but I

swatted his hand away.

"Oh, please. It was cute. Like those funny videos of cats online that overreact when they get spooked. Even your hair seemed to stand up on end."

Rather than try to pinch me again, Magnus changed tactics and kissed me instead.

If this was his way of getting me to stop laughing, then I was eager to comply.

"Come on," he said when the kiss ended. "We're still a mess and need to get cleaned up. You've got an apartment upstairs, right? So, you must have a shower of some sort."

I kept him close and planted a few small kisses at the corner of his mouth, enjoying the rough scrape of his stubble against my lips.

"I do, but the showers not very big. We'll have to take turns."

Taking me by the hand, he started leading me toward my apartment.

"I'm sure we can make something work."

His voice was so tender, I regretted having to tell him that that he was going the wrong direction, and the door he was pulling me toward actually led to the basement.

***

In the end we did make it work. My bathroom was small, and only one of us could get in the shower at a time, but that didn't stop Magnus from finding other ways to "help." Mostly his efforts just ended up making a whole new mess, especially when he managed to pull me into bed, which would then require another shower.

Rinse and repeat.

We took so long to "clean up" that the sun had gone down before we were finally decent enough to step out into public. By then, it was too late for us to pursue our investigation further, so we spent the rest of the evening ordering take out and just watching some mindless television.

As much as I liked sex with him, just relaxing together and talking was also nice. It was the kind of domestic scene I could easily get used to, and by the time we went to bed, I felt spoiled with intimacy.

When the next morning rolled around, we made plans to stop by Magnus's property to inform Brody about what we were doing and pick up our camping supplies again for another trip. However, we'd barely taken a few steps out the door before we were interrupted.

"Trent," Lea called as she ran up the sidewalk toward us. "Wait up. Where are you going?"

Magnus and I shared a look, each silently agreeing not to tell my sister our plans. So, I deflected by simply saying, "Oh, just heading back to Magnus's property. Why? What's up?"

"I figured it out." She was so excited that she barely slowed down as she approached and slammed right into me. Only the fact that I was much taller than her kept us both upright.

She didn't even seem to notice that she'd nearly knocked us both to the ground as she grinned up at me.

"I knew the combination of these three flowers was familiar, and I finally remembered where I'd seen it before. Look."

Something was shoved under my nose, so close that I couldn't even see what it was. Taking the object from her, I held it out to a more reasonable distance and found myself holding a small gold ring.

At first glance it didn't appear noteworthy. To anyone else, it would even seem like a particularly underwhelming piece of jewelry since it had no gemstone or glittering embellishments. The entire ring was made to look like three flowers woven together. I double checked with Magnus, just to be sure, but I wasn't surprised when he confirmed that the flowers were rose, lisianthus, and poppy.

Taking the ring from her, I turned the ring over in my hands. My antique-dealer's eye immediately gauged the ring to be about the same age as the locket, and maybe even crafted by the same artist. It had no gems, but it was still obviously expensive. Based on its weight, it was made of solid gold rather than just the gold plating that a lot of gold rings were made from.

"Where did you get this?"

Lea's answer was not what I expected.

"When Nana died, she left a few things to me. I kept most of it in storage since I had no real use for it. Especially since I travel around so much. This ring was one of the things she gave me."

"Why?"

MAGNUS

I wasn't even sure what I meant by the question. It felt selfish to ask why our grandmother had given an antique like this to my sister and not to me. Of course, my sister deserved to inherit some things from our grandparents as well.

Yet, why hadn't Grandma at least told me about it?

Lea also seemed baffled by the gift of the ring and stared at it like it was as alien specimen.

"I don't know why she gave it to me. I'm not exactly the delicate jewelry wearing type." For emphasis, she gestured to her current outfit, which consisted of her customary leather jacket, matching leather boots, and a few pieces of chunky black-iron jewelry. "I remember her showing it to me once before she died, and she said that it was meant to be passed down the female side of the family. Back then, I didn't realize she was hinting that the ring would pass on to me, and after she died it was too late to ask her."

Lea was several years younger than me, though she often bossed me around like she was the older sibling. When our grandparents had passed, I'd been an adult, but Lea had only been a teenager. While I wished she'd asked more questions, at the time, the trials of high school were probably more important than an old unwanted ring.

Not sure what to make of all this, I just handed the ring back to her.

"It's interesting, but it doesn't really help us. Magnus and I need to get going, so—"

She cut me off before I could finish, grabbing my arm and pulling me in the opposite direction down the road away from where Magnus had parked his truck.

"Do you really have so little faith in me. Of course I couldn't leave it at just that. I want answers, too, so I called Nana's old friend. You remember Aunt

Missy, right?"

I did, though I hadn't seen the woman in a long time. When I was a child, she'd been like a second grandmother to me, but age kept her mostly housebound now, and life had kept me too busy to visit.

Thinking about it now, I regretted that I hadn't seen her in so long. Aunt Missy may not actually be related to me, but she was one of the few links left to my grandparents other than their store.

I shook off Lea's hand on my arm and followed her willingly. Magnus, bless him, didn't say a word as he came along as well. We must have made for a strange sight, two large men following behind a shorter woman like obedient ducklings, but luckily no one stopped us or tried to talk to us along the way.

It was still early in the morning. Most people were either in a hurry to get to work, or too tired to bother with conversation.

Emberwood was a small town, with most of its important buildings sitting along one main road. Some people, like Magnus, chose to live farther out in the woods, but many had built their homes near the center of town for convenience. Aunt Missy was one of these people, and her little cottage was only a few minutes' walk away.

I'd forgotten how close she lived, and as we stepped up to her front door, I felt even more shame over not visiting her more. Even with my old leg injury, which twinged every now and then, I had no excuse. If I could hike through the woods for several days with Magnus, then I could have still made the ten-minute walk down a flat road.

Lea barely managed to finish knocking before the door was thrown open.

The woman who greeted us was exactly as I remembered, but also different in a few ways. She still wore her hair in a messy bun that sat loosely on the nape of her neck like it would unravel at any moment, and still dressed in ridiculously beaded shawls that clinked together every time she moved. Yet, there was also more lines creasing her dark skin, and a hollowness to her cheeks that I didn't remember, and her back curved more drastically under the weight of her long life.

She was over ninety years old. If anything, I should have been happy that she was still alive, but instead, I was merely surprised to see she that had aged.

"There you kids are," she greeted us, pulling both Lea and I into a hug with an unexpected amount of strength for her thin arms. "Lea, you called to say that you were coming over, but it's been so long I was starting to get worried something had happened."

When the hug finally ended, Lea rolled

her eyes.

"I only called you twenty minutes ago."

Clicking her tongue at us, Aunt Missy herded us all inside. "At my age, you can never be too careful. Twenty minutes could be twenty minutes too long. Oh, hello. Who's this?" She finally noticed Magnus, eyeing him up and down with an expression that seemed more appropriate for a strip club. "Lea. Are you finally bringing a man home? You certainly picked a strong looking one."

"No, Aunt Missy," Lea sighed shooting me an apologetic look. "He's a friend of Trent's."

"Well, that's perfect. If he already gets along with your brother, then you know he must be a good man."

Lea sighed again, and this time I joined her.

Magnus accepted Aunt Missy's appraisal with grace and held out his hand to greet her. "Magnus McGuire. I've only been living in town for a few months, so I'm sorry we haven't had a chance to meet sooner, ma'am."

Instead of shaking his hand, Aunt Missy wrapped herself around his entire arm and used it to pull him into the house.

"Handsome and a gentleman. You remind me of my late husband. Lea, you really shouldn't let an opportunity to snag a man like this go to waste."

I bit my tongue to keep what I wanted to say behind my teeth. Yes, Magnus was a good man, and I should be able to brag about "snagging" him. However, I'd never discussed the concept of homosexuality with Aunt Missy, and I had no idea what her opinion would be.

This didn't seem like the time to roll the dice on possible homophobia.

We were all directed to take a seat in the living room, perched on old vintage chairs that didn't seem strong enough to support Magnus or I. Even Lea, with her short but muscular frame, looked a bit uncertain about the chair under her.

Aunt Missy had shared my grandparents' love for antiques, and it showed in the decor around us. Everything in the house was old and delicate. Even the tea set she brought out for us to drink from was ridiculously small and dainty. When she handed me a cup, and I had to pinch the handle between two fingers, barely daring to touch the thing for fear of crushing it in my hands.

It was as she was handing out the teacups to everyone that I noticed a glint of gold on her finger. There, sitting right on her hand, was a ring identical to the one Lea had shown me.

Looking over at Lea, I gestured with my eyes toward the ring. She'd seen it, too, and after taking a polite sip of tea, she pulled out her own ring.

"Aunt Missy. When I called you earlier, I asked about the ring that Nana left me. She never told me much about it, but you've got an identical one as well, so it must have some significance, right?"

"Ah, yes," Aunty Missy rubbed the ring on her finger as she sat in her own chair. "There was once a time when every family in Emberwood had one of these rings, though I see them less and less nowadays. Usually, they are only inherited through the female side of a family line, but..." She glanced for a moment between Magnus and I before seeming to come to a decision. "I suppose it wouldn't hurt if a few more people knew about it. So, few people remember anymore."

I carefully set my teacup down on its saucer, making sure not to let the fragile porcelain clink together. "Aunt Missy, the specific flowers on those rings. Do they have anything to do with Rose,

Lisianthus, and Poppy Milford?"

She seemed surprised that I knew the names of the three sisters, but rather than get upset, she merely looked down at her ring and ran her thumb over the gold flowers with fondness.

"Yes, it does. The Milford family founded this town before it was even known as Emberwood. My great-grandmother lived at the same time as they did, and she told me all about it when this ring passed to me. Rose, Lisianthus, and Poppy are the *Mothers of the Mountain,* and this ring is a symbol for those of us who still uphold their worship."

"Worship?" Lea said, asking the very question that had been on the tip of my tongue. "You make them sound like some sort of gods."

"No, not gods," Aunt Missy shook her head, still caressing her ring. "But those three sisters weren't ordinary mortals either."

Her expression shifted to something stronger, and for a moment the lines of her life seemed to disappear from her face as she looked at us with unwavering conviction.

"They were witches."

CHAPTER ELEVEN

Magnus

"WITCHES?" I STARED at the woman, who Trent had called Aunt Missy, with a skeptical look.

"Yes," Aunt Missy said with such conviction that I instinctually reconsidered my own skepticism. "You heard me. Witches. The real deal, no question." Although her words sounded insane, she spoke with such authority that anyone would easily believe her. It was a miracle the woman never went into politics, or she would have probably ended up as President of the entire country.

There was a clink of porcelain as both Lea and Trent set their teacups down gently.

"Um, Aunt Missy," Lea said hesitantly. "I don't think, um... Do you mean that's what people back then used to think about these sisters."

"Yes." Aunt Missy nodded, still rubbing at her ring. For a second, I thought we'd made progress with her, until she continued. "The townsfolk thought that because that's what they were. Witches. Don't roll your eyes at me, you brats. I know exactly what I'm talking about."

I'd been very careful to keep my expression neutral, so I was certain she wasn't talking about me, but when I glanced over at Lea and Trent, they both had guilty looks on their faces like they'd been caught misbehaving.

Neither sibling seemed to know what to say, so I took control of the conversation for them.

"Um, Aunt Missy—do you mind if I call you that?"

She took a sip of her own tea, smiling at me. "Of course not. These two may not be my actual niece and nephew, but they're as good as. So, you may as well call me Aunt as well if you're going to be part of the family someday."

For a moment, I thought she'd seen through my relationship with Trent, but then I noticed she was glancing toward Lea instead. It seemed she was still stuck on the assumption that everyone in the room was straight, but there was no point in correcting her. It wasn't a malicious assumption. Just an ignorant one born from a different generation. I was often guilty of making such assumptions myself, so I wasn't going to fault her for it.

"Right—um, Aunt Missy. Maybe you

can explain more about what you mean by witches. Surely, you don't mean like with magic and wand waving and stuff."

She waved her hand as if batting away a fly, and the ring on her finger caught the light in such a way so that for a moment it seemed to be made of living flame.

"Oh, nothing like what they show on T.V. now. I've seen those Harold Potter movies, and it's nothing like that. No. I'm talking real witches."

"And what are real witches?"

"Well..." She trailed off and thought for a moment. "My Great Grandmother told me about the day they arrived in town, and apparently, it was obvious they were witches from day one."

Having gotten over her embarrassment at being called out for disrespect, Lea suddenly piped up. "Arrived? You mean the Milford sisters weren't born here?"

Aunt Missy took another sip of tea,

then set her cup aside and sat more comfortably back in her chair like she was preparing for a long story.

"That's right. Those three just showed up in town one day. Strolled right out of the woods like they'd been born from the trees themselves. They were barely out of their teens at the time, and simply asked for a place to stay for a little while. In return, they said they could fix the bad harvest that the town was experiencing at the time. Low and behold, after a single season, the crop fields were already turning out better crops. The Milford family quickly adopted them, and after that, the town seemed to be blessed. Everything that those girls said came true. They even predicted the fire that burned down the town and warned everyone so they could evacuate. The only people that died were the ones who didn't heed the warning."

I didn't say it out loud, but these so-called witches sounded like they probably had a logical explanation. Helping with a bad harvest would be simple for someone with a good knowledge of plants.

Perhaps knowledge, to those who lacked education, might seem like education, but it didn't mean the sisters in question were truly magical.

Lea and Trent must have thought the same as me, for although I could still see the doubt in their eyes, neither of them tried to argue with Aunt Missy.

"All right, so they were witches," Lea said. "The people of the town must have been really grateful for their help."

"Oh, they were," Aunt Missy agreed. "They were known as the *Mothers of the Mountain*. Most of the townsfolk practically worshiped them, though, of course, there were always those who seek to cause trouble. There was a small group of people who thought the *Mothers of the Mountain* were actually demons and tried to get rid of them.”

Beside me, Trent leaned back in his chair with a sigh and stared up at the ceiling. “Let me guess. The Thornley family were some of the people who thought they were demons.”

“They were certainly the most outspoken against the *Mothers of the Mountain*,” Aunt Missy agreed. “They were constantly harassing the Milford family and trying to convince people to ‘cast the demons out of their town’. It didn’t work, but they had enough supporters that they were never fully silenced either. Until Jacob Thornley went missing. That pretty much put an end to their harassment, since he was the unspoken leader of the protests.”

We’d finally come to the true heart of the matter. All this talk of witches and premonitions was just a distraction from the important issues.

Did the body found on my property

belong to Jacob Thornley or not?

I probably shouldn't have been so invested. No matter whose body it turned out to be, I hadn't killed and buried them, so it didn't affect me. Yet, as the one who'd literally dug the coffin out of the ground, I couldn't help but feel invested. Plus, now that people were harassing me about the body and the items found with it, I'd like to at least know why I was being harassed.

"You said Jacob Thornley disappeared, but did they ever figure out what happened to him?"

Aunt Missy had to stop and think for a minute, taking another sip from her rapidly cooling tea as she contemplated an answer she probably hadn't considered before.

"My Great Grandmother never mentioned what happened to that man or why he disappeared. From the sounds of it, the man wasn't really missed. The

Mothers of the Mountain were his main target of harassment, but not his only one. A search was done, but no one outside of his immediate family looked very hard. Some people just aren't happy unless they're making other people miserable, but that kind of life catches up with you sooner or later."

While we'd been talking, the patch of sunlight streaming in through the window had slowly crept its way across the floor. Based on the current angle, it was probably around noon or maybe even a little later. It only felt like a few minutes had passed, but we'd been there longer than it seemed.

"What happened to the sisters?"

I didn't think about the question before I asked it, but Aunt Missy didn't understand what I meant, so I had to elaborate. "*The Mothers of the Mountain?* What eventually happened to them?"

Finally realizing what I meant, Aunt

Missy chuckled. "Oh, honey. Nothing. They may have been witches, but they were still human. They lived, they got old, and eventually, they died. That's it. End of story."

That may have been the end of Aunt Missy's information, but I doubted it was the end of the overall story. While it was looking more and more certain that the body found under my future greenhouse was the remains of Jacob Thornley, it still didn't explain the objects that we'd found in the coffin, or why they'd been buried together in the first place.

When we finally left Aunt Missy's place, it was even later than I'd expected. Noon had already passed, and the sun was already starting the second half of its journey across the sky.

As we walked back to Trent's shop from Aunt Missy's place, we discussed what to do next. It wasn't really a question. Aunt Missy's info had explained a few things but hadn't really given us the answers we were looking for. So, the only thing we could do next was to follow Creed's suggestion and head back out to the hidden mausoleum, following the path on the map exactly and starting at the old mill.

It was simply a matter of how we were going to go about this.

While it was too late to start the trip today, we did toy with the idea of spending the remaining daylight exploring the old mill to see what made the location so important. However, we eventually decided against that. Not knowing what we would find, it would be best to spend the rest of the day gathering supplies and getting ready for the journey before heading out to the old mill.

At the shop, Trent and I parted ways with Lea. She wanted to come with us, but we didn't know exactly how long the trip would take and she needed to leave in a few days for her next volunteer job. Instead, we promised to keep in touch and tell her what we discovered.

Once she'd left and it was just Trent and I, our hands naturally found each other, and our fingers laced together.

"Come on," I said, tugging him toward the door to the shop. "Let's grab whatever you need and meet back up with Brody. We've got a lot to get ready."

We'd already visited the mausoleum once, so the trip shouldn't be too hard. It was just going to be a little longer and we'd start from a different place.

Yet, I couldn't help feeling like there was a long, arduous journey ahead of us, and that no amount of preparation would ever be enough.

***

Upon arriving back at my own property, we found another surprise waiting for us.

"What the hell happened," I said as I

stepped out of my truck, staring gobsmacked around the property.

"I already told you," Brody shouted down from up on top of a ladder where he was hammering another beam into place. "I ain't listening to you two another night, but its still safer for all of us to stay together right now until we get the situation settled. If that means I gotta single-handedly get your house built so you two horny fuckers can have some privacy, then so be it."

As much as I wanted to protest his claim of single-handedly building my house, I couldn't. I'd been helping out, but somehow, over the course of a single night, Brody had made more progress getting my house finished than I had in a month.

It certainly wasn't done. No one looking at the structure would call it a house. However, there were a few fully enclosed rooms and a temporary roof in place that was enough to make the structure habitable.

"Did you pull an all-nighter to get this done," I asked as I ran a hand over one of the newly erected walls. It was perfectly smooth and sanded, with not even enough gap between the joints to fit a piece of paper.

"I got plenty of sleep, don't worry," Brody said as he finished hammering in the last nail. While Brody rarely lied, he did often bend the truth for the sake of convenience. The fact that he wouldn't look me in the eye when he spoke meant that, while he had gotten some sleep, it wasn't nearly as much as he was implying.

The man had probably gotten plenty of use out of his fancy coffee machine last night.

Knowing better than to argue with Brody when he was in the mood to be difficult, I let it go.

"All right. Well, come on down so we can tell you what we found while we were in town. I think we're going to have to plan another trip out to that mausoleum."

Over the course of a very late lunch, Trent and I explained everything, including the newspaper articles, Creed's observations about the map, and Aunt Missy's story. In the end, as I suspected, Brody agreed with Creed that we should try following the path of the map this time to see if we could find anything new. At this point, we were starting to hit a dead end for leads and were running out of ideas. If another trip out to the mausoleum didn't reveal anything, we might have to resign ourselves to never fully knowing the secret of the body we'd found.

Such a fate wouldn't be the end of the world, so long as people stopped harassing us, but the lack of answers would bother me, like a splinter in my mind I'd never be able to get out.

Just like before, Brody would stay here to keep up the illusion that we weren't doing anything unusual, just in case we were still being watched, while Trent and I took a hike through the woods. With a plan in place, Brody started gathering supplies for us, while I focused on moving my stuff into my own house.

Since only a few rooms were complete, it felt more like a studio apartment than a house, with just enough space for a bedroom and bathroom. The unfinished parts of the structure stood around the completed rooms like a promise of the house that was to come, reminding me of a living heart surrounded by a protective ribcage. It wasn't perfect, but it was good enough for Trent and I to have some privacy.

We were planning on leaving for our trip back to the hidden mausoleum tomorrow, and we could have just slept in the guest room at Brody's house for one more night, but since we would probably be busy for the next few days, I wanted one more night of privacy. Our earlier plan to stay at Trent's apartment had ended up with us being interrupted multiple times. Privacy was in short supply, and we weren't going to pass up any opportunity we could get.

As Trent and I were moving my stuff out of Brody's guestroom and into the finished bedroom in my house, I realized I'd accrued more junk than I realized. Some of it, I'd even forgotten about completely.

When Trent pulled out a cardboard box from the back of the closet, I had no idea what it was at first. Then I read the name on the shipping label, and my stomach dropped.

"Wait, not that."

I lunged for the box, but it was too late.

Trent pulled out the contents and held them up in confusion for both of us to see.

"What..." he started to ask, but then stopped.

The item in his hands was obvious.

It had been an impulse purchase when I bought the lingerie and had immediately second-guessed myself the moment I had it in my hands. Rather than go through the embarrassment of returning it, I'd shoved it to the back of my closet and forgotten about it. Out of sight, out of mind. I'd never expected it to come back to haunt me, but the embarrassment I felt as I saw the construction of blue lace and silk in Trent's hands was a hundred times worse than the anonymous embarrassment I would have felt from just returning it.

"Umm..." I stuttered as I tried to think of what to say. "That's not mine. I mean, it is, but, like, it's not for me. I just thought I might give it to a partner someday."

Trent nodded but didn't say anything as he rubbed the material between his fingers, exploring the thin delicate design.

"So... you like this kind of thing?"

I shrugged, unable to look him in the eye as my face burned. "It looks nice, and I thought it seemed well made."

Trent was clearly uncomfortable and there was a deep crease between his brows that revealed his thoughts weren't pleasant. He obviously didn't like the idea of the lingerie. Before it could upset him anymore, I snatched it out of his hands and shoved it into the nearest half-filled bag so neither of us had to look at it any longer.

"It was just a silly idea I had months ago. I forgot all about it. It's not a requirement or anything, so don't worry about it."

Trent didn't say anything more about

the lingerie, but he was also strangely quiet as we finished packing and moved the bulk of my stuff to the bedroom in my own house. Even during dinner that night, as we were planning for our upcoming hiking trip, he remained lost in his own thoughts.

It was going to take us a lot longer to hike out to the secret mausoleum from the old mill than the path we'd taken before, so there was more to prepare. Because of this, I didn't have an opportunity to talk to Trent about his shift in attitude. Something was clearly bothering him, but I wasn't sure what.

Surely, the fact that I'd impulsively bought a set of lingerie couldn't have upset him that much. If it was something left over from an ex, I might have understood, but they were completely unused. The tag had even still been on, revealing that I'd paid far too much for something that was just shoved to the back of my closet.

I tried to console myself with the idea that maybe whatever was bothering him had nothing to do with the lingerie, and the timing was just a coincidence.

It didn't work.

Even as I repeated this idea to myself, I didn't believe a word of what I was thinking.

We spent the rest of the evening with Brody, making sure we had everything we needed for our trip tomorrow. So, it wasn't until much later that night, when Trent and I were alone in the bedroom of my half-finished house, I finally had a chance to talk to him.

"Hey," I said gently, putting my hand on his shoulder as soon as the bedroom door closed and we'd locked it behind us. "You okay? You've been... quiet."

Since the rest of the structure hadn't been finished and the bedroom stood by itself, it was more like a motel than a house. I could hear the outside world just on the other side of the door. Night had fallen, and the forest had gone to sleep with it. Even the trees weren't rustling tonight, and no curious nocturnal creatures were sniffing around the property.

All this lack of noise just emphasized how quiet Trent was. His breathing was the loudest thing in the room. If I concentrated really hard, I could almost hear his heartbeat.

Nearly a full minute passed before he finally spoke.

"Magnus, am I..." He trailed off before he'd barely even started the sentence. A strange, unsettled look flashed through his eye, like something rippling just under the surface of dark waters. Then, without another word, he grabbed my shoulders and kissed me.

I could practically taste the words he hadn't said on his tongue. His kiss was rough and demanding, like he was trying to swallow me whole, and I loved it. Yet, after a moment, he suddenly stopped and pulled away until he was sitting on the bed looking up at me.

"We're going to be busy for a few days. We should take advantage of tonight while we can."

He moved himself further onto the bed until he was lying on his back, beckoning with an obvious invitation.

Whatever he failed to say earlier was completely forgotten as I eagerly grabbed the supplies stashed in one of my bags and then joined him on the bed.

If our relationship continued, once we had some free time, I'd have to ask Trent about the two of us getting tested so we could get rid of the condoms. I'd love to indulge in his body without any barrier between us. However, for now, we played it safe.

Our clothing was quickly scattered

across the floor. Since the room had been specifically designed for me, the bed was more than big enough for both Trent and me. We had room to spare, but I still pressed close as I kneeled over him, looking down at his body spread below me.

The wall sconce lights attached over the bed were meant more for ambiance than actually lighting, so the entire room was cast in a romantic glow that softened the edges between light and shadow. It gave a warm hue to Trent's fair skin, and highlighted the freckles scattered over his shoulders. Every inch of him looked soft and inviting, but when I ran my hands over him, there was deliciously hard core under soft flesh.

His stomach was a particular delight, and I couldn't help grabbing it with both hands. Like most athletes, he had a strong core, but there was also a healthy amount of softness clinging to his hips and stomach. According to him, many serious weightlifters carried some extra weight around the middle. It gave them more energy and allowed them to push their bodies to the limits of their strength.

I loved it.

Moving up from his stomach, I slid my hands over his chest. Even with the fingers of both hands spread to their limit, I couldn't encompass the entire width of his broad chest. The muscles there were especially well developed and fit perfectly against the curve of my palms.

Squeezing his chest, I felt both nipples under my palms harden into little, tight pebbles. A nipple ring would look really good on him. As I continued groping him, listening to his soft moans, I toyed with the idea of a few different ideas. Eventually, I decided he would look best with a rich yellow-gold ring embellished by either a blue or green gem. The metal would complement the natural gold tones in his skin, while the bright gem would contrast with his dark chest hair and make it stand out even more.

Arousal throbbed heavily between my legs as I pictured it and I leaned down to take one of his nipples into my mouth. Even without the embellishment of jewelry, his body was still a delight to my senses. His scent, musky with the smell of sex and pleasure, went right to my head and made me moan.

Trent gasped and writhed against the bed. One of his hands tangled in my hair.

"Are you just going to tease me all night, or are you going to get on with it?" He said the words, but at the same time his hand in my hair pressed my head closer and encouraged the attention of my mouth.

I could have spent the whole night just worshiping this part of him, but I had other plans and only so many hours before sunrise.

When I finally managed to pull my mouth away from him, I sat up to find his legs already wrapped around me. His hips jerked and his flushed cock was leaking all over his stomach. It almost looked like he'd already found his release, but I knew we weren't there yet.

I barely even thought about what I was doing as I automatically applied a condom to myself. I couldn't bear to look away from the sight that Trent made, and it was more luck than skill that ensured the condom was applied properly.

The lube was a different matter. That, I took my time with. After liberally coating my fingers, I slowly inserted one inside him, watching various emotions play over his face the whole time. There was a slight pinch around his eyes when my finger first pressed inside, hinting at the pain he felt as his internal muscles stretched, but the discomfort clearly didn't last long and was soon replaced by pleasure. When I added a second finger, I moved even slower than before, but this time I knew by the look of bliss on his features that there was no pain at all. I moved more freely, pressing deeper into him and scissoring my fingers to coax his muscles to open.

I knew the moment I hit his good spot. His whole body tensed and his back arched, yet the tight rim of his hole loosened even more, practically inviting me inside.

A third finger joined the first two. I spent some time just letting my fingers slide in and out of him, and in just a few minutes, he was a sweating, panting wreck. Trent's dark eyes glazed over as he stared up at me and he muttered a few barely coherent words begging me to hurry up.

I obliged.

Adding a little more lube to my cock, I grabbed both of Trent's legs and spread them wider so I could line myself up with him.

We'd already slept together several times, in a variety of positions, but when I pressed inside him and felt the heat of his body tight around me, it was just as thrilling as the first time. At first, I'd intended to take it slow, teasing him while savoring him at the same time. That idea went right out the window the moment his thighs squeezed my waist and he started bucking his hips, too, practically fucking himself on me.

Trent was desperate, and he pulled me along for the ride.

Bracing my hands against the bed, I started up a punishing pace, pulling almost all the way out and then immediately slamming back inside. The headboard knocked against the newly erected wall with the force of each thrust, and I silently praised Brody's constructions skills for building such a solid structure. I probably would have knocked down the wall otherwise.

My mind was lost in a white haze of pleasure as Trent seemed to be all around me at once. I buried my face against his neck as my hips seemed to move on their own, unable to be controlled. I gripped Trent hard enough to leave bruises on his skin, but he didn't protest. Based on his moans and whimpered pleading, he even liked the rough handling.

Something hot and electric coiled tighter and tighter in my stomach, growing more intense each time I plunged back inside Trent. I couldn't even call it pleasure any more. The combination of so many sensations surpassed such a simple classification.

Was there a word for something greater than pleasure?

Greater than ecstasy?

Maybe. However, I wasn't a skilled enough wordsmith to think of anything.

MAGNUS

The final straw was when Trent gripped my face in his hands and pulled me into a kiss. It was such a gentle, chaste gesture. A startling contrast to the raw passion flowing between us. Such a delicate touch only made everything else seem even more intense by comparison, and the tightening in my gut snapped. My orgasm hit me with the force of a sledgehammer, and I groaned deeply into the kiss as I pressed as deeply into his tight heat as possible.

At the same time, I drifted one of my hands down to wrap around Trent's arousal that was trapped between us. It only took a few strokes to finish him off as well. His legs wrapped tighter around me, and he gripped my hair so hard my scalp tingled as heat flooded between us.

Through it all, our lips never parted.

It took a few minutes, but eventually, I broke free of the haze of orgasm enough to form a few coherent thoughts. I wanted to just collapse, exhausted, onto the bed, but I kept myself upright by bracing my arms against the mattress. My hands shook as I reached down to remove myself from Trent while keeping the condom in place; then I removed it and properly disposed of it in the nearby trashcan.

Trent lay over the bed, arms and legs spread in all directions. He looked wrecked, and a sense of pride settled in my chest.

I'd done that. I'd satisfied my partner so well that he was practically catatonic afterward. It was an ego boost I didn't even know I needed. If I'd looked in a mirror at that moment, I probably would have been glowing with confidence.

Although I was also exhausted, I first slipped off to the bathroom to fetch a wet towel to clean us both up. A shower would have been better, but I was ready to collapse, and Trent didn't look like he'd be capable of moving any time soon. A quick wipe down with the towel would have to do. We could take a shower in the morning, though I doubted we'd have time for anything fun. A busy day waited for us tomorrow and we would need to get an early start.

I probably should have been worrying about the journey ahead of us, but I felt nothing but contentment as I slipped into the extra-large bed beside Trent, turned off the light, and drifted off to sleep with the weight of his legs casually tangled with mine.

CHAPTER TWELVE

Trent

THE OLD MILL was... well, a mill.

I wasn't sure what I expected, but after so much importance had been given to the structure, I'd pictured something grander. Something more deserving of all the effort we'd gone to recently.

As Magnus and I stood within the empty interior of the building, looking around at the high ceiling and cavernous space, I was sadly disappointed. The building was old enough to no longer be usable, but not old enough to be truly interesting. The only noteworthy thing about it was how sturdy the stone walls had been built. Since it was a mill, it had naturally been built next to a river to power the waterwheel that was used to turn the millstone. After a hundred and twenty-five years, the wooden wheel had rotted away long ago, but the stone walls were still surprisingly sturdy. They barely looked like they shifted over the decades, despite the proximity to running water.

"There's nothing here," I said. My voice echoed back at me, like the building itself was agreeing.

Magnus wasn't so easily dissuaded and looked around the hollowed-out building with much more eager eyes.

"The mill may not be important. It's might have just been the most convenient starting point for the map's path, but let's take a closer look first before we move on."

MAGNUS

Withholding my complaints, I heaved a sigh, hitched my bag higher onto my back, and followed him.

I'd been in a bad mood since waking up that morning. Having Magnus in the bed next to me should have been a great way to start the day, but I couldn't shake the black cloud that hung over my head and prickled at my skin with the static of discontent. Something felt knotted in my chest, and I didn't know why.

So far, my plan to just ignore it wasn't working, but I didn't know what else to do.

The old mill was bigger than it initially seemed. Behind the main building, where most of the work had once been done, there was a series of smaller stone houses connected by a series of courtyards. Without furniture or identifying markers, it was hard to tell what the smaller houses were meant for. They seemed too lavish to just be storage, and their distance from the main building would have been inconvenient.

"Look here," Magnus called from the empty doorway of one of the houses. "I think this pile of wood was once a bed. It kinda looks like a frame."

It looked more like a pile of sticks, but the general size of the structure seemed about right for a bed.

"So, people lived here?" I asked, picking up one of the wooden planks that was still in good condition. One end had been carved to look like a lion's foot. The design was common for the legs of furniture, making Magnus's conclusion about it being a bed even more likely. "Maybe these were homes for the workers of the mill."

"Maybe," Magnus said, but I could tell from his tone that he wasn't convinced. He stepped over to the house's window, where the river was still clearly visible. "Milford. We assumed the family was named that because they built the mill. But maybe they built the mill here because they already lived on this part of the land."

"So, you think these were the family's homes?"

"It would explain why they're all connected by courtyards. They kept expanding as the family grew, and eventually, set their sights to harnessing the river."

"Okay." I agreed that it did make sense, though I still didn't see why Magnus was making such a big deal out of it. "But that doesn't really tell us anything."

When Magnus looked back at me, he was smiling. The early morning light reflected in his blue eyes, making them sparkle just like reflections off the river.

"Rose, Lisianthus, and Poppy were adopted by the Milford family, right? Then they might have lived here as well. If we can figure out exactly where they lived, we might be able to find something."

It seemed like a difficult, and potentially fruitless task, but when Magnus smiled at me like that, I would have agreed to anything.

After an hour of carefully searching each of the connected houses, we did eventually stumble upon something promising. The very last house in the group had a larger courtyard than the rest. We had to pull several layers of ivy off the walls just to get through the front door, but when we did, we discovered a carving of three familiar flowers above the doorframe.

"Well," I said, looking up at the image of a rose, lisianthus, and poppy flower woven together into an eternal wreath. "That looks promising."

Inside, the house was also larger than the others, with three distinct living areas instead of just one. It also had a back door, which led to a patch of land overrun with a variety of plants. I didn't recognize them, but Magnus of course did. He probably could have spent the entire day just examining this one area.

According to him, the combination of plants behind the house weren't naturally inclined to grow together, and many of them weren't native to the area. The land was completely overgrown now and looked no different than any other patch of greenery, but Magnus was certain that the spot had once been a garden, and I had to agree with him.

It was so easy to picture. Three sisters, living a humble life in this little house, tending their garden and assisting with the running of the mill.

So, what had changed?

How did they go from the modest life left behind in this small house to literal figures of worship?

Clearing away some of the overgrown

plants revealed a path of steppingstones leading from the backdoor of the house to the other side of the garden. Since this house sat at the very edge of the mill's property, it butted up against the wall surrounding the whole area. The steppingstone path led to an archway built into the wall, with climbing ivy draped over both sides like natural curtains.

Beyond those ivy curtains lay the untamed forest of the mountain.

Pulling aside the vines with one hand, Magnus gestured me through. "After you."

The archway was short, so even with his assistance, I had to duck my head as I passed through the ivy curtain.

On the other side of the archway, a steppingstone path stretched into the forest and disappeared among the shade of the trees. Magnus double-checked his satellite GPS device and compared it to a picture of the map we'd found in Rose's locket.

Neither of us were surprised to find that the steppingstone path led exactly in the direction we needed to go.

"So, do we just follow the path?" I asked as we stood at the edge of the tree line.

Magnus scowled down at his GPS, as if waiting for it to give him a different answer. "I guess. Everything certainly seems to be leading us in this way."

Despite its age, the steppingstone path was surprisingly well preserved. The roots of nearby trees seemed unwilling to grow near the stones, so the path still sat flat and undisturbed. We had to stop a few times to brush away grass and dirt to make sure we were still on the path, but overall, it was a relatively easy walk.

At first, even after entering the forest, I could still make out the top of the mill's roof through the canopy, but with every step I took it grew harder and harder to see. Just as the rushing sound of the river completely disappeared from my ears, the path abruptly zigzagged to the side around a large boulder.

On the other side of the boulder stood another archway, identical to the one we'd passed through before, but this one wasn't part of a wall. It stood alone, supported only by a pair of trees on either side, and looked completely out of place among the natural landscape of the forest.

We stopped in front of the archway, and Magnus pinched a few leaves from the curtain of vines that grew on this structure as well.

"These vines are different. It's not the same kind of ivy as the other archway."

"Does that matter?" I asked, peering at the leaves in his hands. They looked the same to me, but I didn't have his eye for plants. "Wait... they're not poisonous, are they?"

"Noooooo," Magnus dragged out the word like he expected a long sentence to follow and was surprised with no other words came.

I waited for a moment to see if he had anything else to say, but he just kept staring at the leaves and inspecting the seemingly harmless vine.

"Well, if it's same, then we should probably get going," I suggested, very conscious of our minimal daylight. The journey would be even longer than our trip before. Several days at least, and it was already approaching midday now. We were going to be out in this forest forever if we kept stopping to inspect every interesting plant.

Without a word, Magnus shrugged but nodded his agreement and held the vines aside for me to pass under the archway. We could have just gone around since there was no wall here, but the path led through the archway, so through the archway we went.

Once again, I had to duck to fit under the short structure, but this time when I straightened up and looked back, Magnus was nowhere in sight.

"Magnus?" I called, turning in circles as I looked for him. I got no answer and saw no sign of him. There weren't even footprints to mark where he'd been standing.

He was gone, and I was alone.

***

Magnus wasn't the only thing that was missing. After looking around, I realized I didn't recognize the area at all. The trees were different. I may not be an expert when it came to plants, but even I could recognize the difference between an oak and a pine tree.

It was like I'd suddenly found myself in a completely different part of the forest.

The archway was also gone, replaced

by a solid stone wall. It resembled the wall that surrounded the mill's property, but this one was much taller. The mill's wall had barely stood taller than me. I could easily reach up and touch the top of the wall. Now, even if I jumped, I couldn't grab the top, and my efforts to climb the wall proved useless. My hands and feet seemed to slip off the surface almost immediately and sent me crashing back to the ground each time.

Panic clawed at my chest, and my breathing came in short erratic bursts.

"Magnus, this isn't funny! Answer me!"

My demands were met with only silence and the natural sounds of the forest.

Maybe I should have stayed put, but in that moment, I couldn't just sit around and wait for something to happen.

When someone was lost, the usual advice was to stay in one place and wait for rescue, but did that still apply here?

I wasn't even sure which of us was the lost one.

Was I lost, or was he?

The forest was darker than it should have been for midday. I considered leaving the path and heading out into the forest directly, hoping to maybe find a way around the wall. However, the moment my foot touched down on the ground beyond the path, the hair on the back of my neck stood up and a foreboding chill ran up my spine.

I'd heard people talk about the sensation of "feeling like someone just stepped on my grave" but before that moment I didn't fully understand what that meant.

Now I did. It was a perfect description of the inexplicable dread that I felt.

Leaving the path wasn't an option.

Not knowing what else to do, I traveled down the steppingstone path away from the wall. The pack on my back made running impossible, so I walked as quickly as I could bear. After only a few minutes my legs were already sore and I felt exhausted. I'd barely made any progress, but I already felt like I needed to sit down.

I compromised by leaning against a tree as I took a drink of water and shook some feeling back into my legs.

This wasn't normal. None of it was normal, but I couldn't stop moving.

The water helped, and my panic settled enough for me to think with a bit more clarity. I pulled out my phone—something I should have done from the start—but I wasn't surprised to find I had no signal.

At that point, nothing would have surprised me.

Or so I thought.

A few minutes later, I was proven wrong.

I'd just started walking again, when I was startled by the sound of footsteps.

They walked when I walked, and stopped when I stopped, but they definitely weren't mine, and always seemed to be just a few steps behind me. I quickly turned around to try and catch whoever was stalking me but found nothing but an empty path no matter which way I looked.

I was so busy looking around for the source of the footprints, I never noticed the sudden break in the path. One moment I was walking along with solid ground under my feet, and the next I stepped out onto open air.

My whole body pitched forward as I fell down a deep ravine. The walls of the ravine were slightly angled, so I rolled and slid my way down to the bottom. I tucked myself into a ball, letting my arms and legs take the brunt of the impact until I finally came to a stop.

The air had been knocked from my lungs and the first few breaths after the fall were difficult. I lay on my back, staring up at the sliver of the canopy I could see above the ravine. I'd fallen a fair distance, and even just looking at the walls of the ravine, I knew I was going to have a hard time climbing out.

Every joint in my body groaned in protest as I clambered back to my feet. It was dark down at the bottom· of the ravine. I could barely see my own feet and kept one hand braced along the wall as I shuffled forward. At some point during my fall, I'd lost my pack with all my supplies. I searched around the nearby ground but found nothing. There weren't even any skid marks in the dirt to mark where the pack may have fallen.

I'd lost Magnus, lost my supplies, and was probably going to lose my sanity soon if this kept up.

There were only two directions to go. Right or left. Both looked identical—meaning I couldn't really see much either way—so I picked the one that seemed to be headed more in the direction I'd initially been heading and started walking.

The ravine stretched on and on, never changing or deviating. I felt like I'd been walking for hours without a single hint that I was getting anywhere. I managed to find the outline of a rock in the dark and sat down, wishing I had still had some water. My throat was parched, and my mouth was dry. Even swallowing made my tongue feel like it was made from sandpaper.

When footsteps echoed in the darkness again, I was too tired to do more than look up.

This time the footsteps were definitely getting closer. They were right on top of me, echoing in my ears, when a figure emerged from the darkness. It was a person, and they were running straight down the ravine.

They never saw me. Never even looked

in my direction. They ran right past me like I wasn't even there.

"Hey, wait," I called as I jumped to my feet, but my voice trailed off when I realized I recognized the person.

It was me.

A younger version of me, specifically. Based on the haircut, I could even identify exactly how old the younger version of me was. I'd only worn that stupid rattail during the sixth grade, when I was trying to imitate a character from a show I'd liked at the time. I couldn't even remember the show anymore, but I remembered the hairstyle.

The younger me ran until a rock came flying out of the shadows and hit him in the back of the head. He fell forward, scraping his hands and forearms over the ground as he caught himself. My own palms and forearms tingled with the memory of injuries that had long since healed.

More rocks bounced off of the younger me's back, keeping him from getting up.

More voices shouted in the darkness.

"Ah ha. Look at him."

"The gorilla's so clumsy."

Several kids, about the same age as the younger me, ran out of the dark and surrounded the figure on the ground. They surrounded him, jeering and taunting, and pushing him back down when he tried to get up.

The younger me lay frozen in a defensive ball on the ground, while my older self-stood several feet away, equally useless.

I remembered this. I wished I could say it was just a bad dream, but I remembered this exact event. It had been a reoccurring scene when I was younger.

I'd hit puberty earlier than the other boys my age and seemed to practically double in size overnight. Unfortunately, my confidence didn't grow with my body, so although I was physically strong, I was emotionally weak, and the other kids knew it. My size, along with my emotional vulnerability, made me the perfect target for their bullying.

"Come on," one of the faceless kids said as they shoved the younger me with their foot. "Fight back. What? Too scared? The big giant's just a big baby."

The faceless bully pulled back their foot like they were getting ready to kick my young self, but before they could make contact, another figure came hurtling out of the darkness.

An even younger version of my sister dove straight at the bully like a linebacker, tackling him to the ground.

"Get away from my brother," she screamed as she struck the kid she'd tackled over and over, bloodying his nose and giving him two impressive black eyes.

The other kids tried to pull her off, but she turned her ferocity on them and bit the nearest one hard enough to break the skin. She looked feral with someone else's blood dripping from her lips, and the other kids started screaming.

Meanwhile, the younger me took the opportunity to clamber off the ground and get out of there, running off into the dark without even looking back.

"Trent, wait," the younger version of Lea called as she ran after me. The other kids followed us, and just like that they'd all disappeared from sight and the adult me was alone once again.

I reached out Mmy hand in the direction they'd gone but grasped nothing but air.

"Wait."

On hesitant steps, I shuffled through the dark after them.

Surely, this wasn't actually happening. I must be hallucinating or something. Or maybe I truly had gone insane. These visions should have been locked away in my memories and only able to haunt me in my dreams, yet here they were right before my waking eyes.

I could still just barely hear the sound of their running footsteps and I trailed after the sound. Yet, the longer I listened the more the sound seemed to shift until I realized I wasn't hearing footsteps at all.

No, it was a much more recognizable sound of weights being repeatedly picked up and put down. It was a sound that was practically drilled into my brain, as familiar as my own heartbeat.

To help solve my bullying problem, my family had started taking me to the local gym so I could build up my confidence. There I'd fallen in love with weightlifting, which eventually led me to competing.

After seeing a younger version of myself right in front of my eyes, I wasn't surprised when I stumbled upon a barbell sitting on the floor of the ravine. I instinctively reached for the bar, but someone beat me to it.

The version of myself that grabbed the bar was still younger, though not as much as the child version of me had been. This version of me was in prime competitive form, with even more pronounced muscles in my arms and legs. The competitive version of me was even wearing the unitard that was standard for weightlifting competitions.

I'd always hated that thing. The tight material clung to every curve of my body and the short hem cut into my thighs each time I moved.

The competitive version of me stood right in front of the bar, taking a ready position for a snatch. It was a particularly difficult move where the lifter dropped into a squat while simultaneously lifting the bar up over their head and holding it there.

It had also once been my best move.

The competitive version of me shifted

on his feet several times before lifting the bar, and I instantly knew something was wrong. I'd always had strong legs and rarely changed my stance once I placed my feet.

Before the competitive version of me even lifted the bar, I knew what I was about to see.

The first half of the snatch was clean, but something went wrong when I dropped into the bottom half of my squat. My feet were unstable, and one of my legs suddenly turned to the side.

This was the competition where I'd been injured. I'd nearly dropped the weight on my head, and only the quick reaction of the competition's spotters kept me from smashing my own brains out.

Watching it now, I could still feel the pain in my knee as both ligaments tore. That was a moment I wasn't going to forget, for it marked the end of my competition days. The injury eventually healed, but the knee would never be as good as new, and I could no longer perform at a competitive level.

The competitive version of me lay on the ground, clutching my injured knee with a look of shock on his face. At the time, I'd been so confused and it wouldn't be until weeks later that I would learn what really happened.

One of the other competitors had sabotaged me.

Most weightlifters wore special shoes that elevated the heel and provided a sturdier base for the foot. Most regular shoes weren't built to support so much weight, and the secret to strong lifting started at the feet.

One of the other competitors had secretly altered my shoes so that my heels were raised to two slightly different heights, which threw off my balance and caused my leg to turn out. When it was discovered, they'd been banned from all competitions, but punishing the person responsible couldn't un-injure my knee. The damage had already been done.

If they'd sabotaged me because they were afraid of me as a competitor, I might have understood their actions to some degree. However, their motivations had nothing to do with my skills as a competitor. They'd sabotaged me simply because they found out I was gay, and they didn't want me "tainting the sport."

The ironic thing was that, upon investigating the event, my saboteur was discovered to be on steroids, making them hypocritical as well as homophobic.

When I'd found out that bit of information, I'd laughed until I'd cried, then promptly drunk myself into a stupor. My sister had eventually found me passed out on my couch and removed all the alcohol from my house.

I couldn't bear to see myself writhing around on the ground in pain anymore, so I walked away from the competitive version of myself and left him behind in the dark.

What was the point of this illusion?

To remind me of all my worst memories?

They were already in my head bothering me every day, and the pain they'd caused had already faded. Though it did leave me wondering where the illusions had come from.

When Aunt Missy had claimed the Milford sisters were witches, I hadn't believed her, but now I couldn't help but wonder.

If these illusions weren't witchcraft, they certainly felt similar.

A light shone off in the distance, faint but getting closer with every step I took. I picked up the pace and started walking faster, hopeful that I'd found the end of this cursed ravine.

No. It was no end at all.

MAGNUS

When I reached the source of the light, I found a large, full-length mirror blocking the entire width of the ravine. It had an antique design, like the kind of thing I'd sell at my shop, and was probably made of real silver-backed glass.

Although I suspected it was an illusion, curiosity got the better of me, and I stepped forward to inspect the mirror. My gaze was first drawn to the intricate craftsmanship of the frame, and I stood appraising it quality and value.

All thoughts of the mirror's craftsmanship fled from my mind when I looked at the glass and saw my own reflection. I wasn't myself.

Or... I was, but not a version of me that I knew.

The version of me in the reflection was smaller, with a more delicate shape. I was still obviously male, but in a more feminine way that was a common stereotype of gay men.

I was also dressed in a set of familiar blue lingerie.

The image in the mirror's reflection looked so realistic, I instinctively looked down at myself to make sure my clothing hadn't spontaneously changed.

No. I was still dressed in my hiking clothes, and my body was still the same burly shape as always. Nothing about me had changed. It was just another illusion.

With the painful memories of my past still fresh in my mind, anger bloomed within me like a bloody flower clogging my throat as I looked at this false reflection.

How much easier would my life have been if that was what I truly looked like?

Ever since I was young, I never felt like enough.

Not strong enough to protect myself from bullies, but not weak enough to inspire protection. It had taken my sister getting suspended for fighting before the adults in my life realized they needed to step in, and even then, all they did was encourage me to fight for myself. Being gay meant I wasn't "masculine" enough for traditionally male spaces like the gym and weightlifting, but I also wasn't feminine enough to fit the image most people expected for someone of my sexuality.

Even the dates I'd managed to find that were interested in a burly gay man balked when they realized I was also interested in "feminine" things like antiques. It was the reason I'd almost never gotten a second date.

To deserve people's approval, I had to be all one thing or another. Either all strong, or all weak. All masculine, or all feminine. Living with one foot on either side of the fence just left me in an awkward, and lonely position that no one knew what to do with.

When I'd first seen the lingerie in Magnus's closet, my first thought was that it looked pretty, and the fabric had been nice to touch. I would have considered wearing it if he asked, but he'd snatched it out of my hands so quickly that it was clear that such an idea wasn't even an option.

Once again, I wasn't enough.

If that was what he wanted, someone who would look good in such an outfit, then what was he doing with me?

As if summoned by my thoughts, Magnus's image appeared in the reflection of the mirror, looking exactly as he had when I last saw him. His arms wrapped around the false reflection of me, and the smaller version of my body easily fit within his embrace.

Magnus and the false reflection of me looked good together, and I hated it. I would never be that person in the mirror.

I didn't want to be that person in the mirror. I just wanted to be me and find someone who liked my contradictions. I'd thought that Magnus could be that person, but if he'd bought that set of lingerie because he wanted his future partner to wear it, then maybe...

Maybe...

No. I wasn't going to let this illusion win.

"Fuck you!" I shouted as I grabbed a rock from the ground. "That's not me. It's never gonna be me, and if that's the kind of partner Magnus really wants, then he can tell me himself. So, fuck off!"

I slammed the rock into the mirror, shattering the false reflection into a hundred splinters of sharp glass. Even the frame collapsed into pieces as if the metal had been nothing stronger than cardboard.

Running past the remains of the broken mirror, I stumbled out of the dark ravine and back into the light of day. I blinked and held up a hand to shield my eyes as my vision adjusted to the light and looked around at the trees surrounding me. I'd once again moved to a different part of the forest, but the steppingstone path still lay beneath my feet and a familiar figure sat on a tree stump not far away.

"Magnus," I shouted as I ran over to him.

He sat hunched over with his head clenched in his hands but looked up at the sound of his name. His expression was completely blank as he looked at me, like I was a stranger to him.

I hesitated when I reached him.

"Magnus? What's wrong?"

My hand gently gripped his shoulder, intending to offer comfort, but the moment I touched him, his face contorted with fury. He pounced like a wild predator, knocking me to the ground and pinning me under his weight.

I couldn't even gasp as his hands wrapped around my throat and squeezed.

CHAPTER THIRTEEN

Magnus

"TRENT?"

My voice was small and fragile, and barely sounded like myself.

His familiar face swam into view, blurry and indistinct. It looked up at me, not with the affection that I'd grown used to, but with terror.

I was lying on top of him with my hands wrapped around his throat.

Throwing myself off of him, my back hit the solid surface of a tree trunk and drove the air right out of my lungs.

Trent turned onto his side, hacking into the dirt as he gasped for breath.

"What..." He struggled to speak as he kept coughing. "Magnus? What the hell?"

I couldn't explain.

How could I possibly tell him that I'd mistaken him for an enemy on the battlefield?

For years, the army had been my life. I was so comfortable in that environment that I hadn't even realized anything was wrong. One moment I'd been hiking through the forest, and the next, I'd been fighting for my life, and my brain never registered the difference.

It wasn't until I felt the give of his throat under my hand that I realized something was wrong. He didn't fight back as I expected or try to get me off of him. All he did was freeze in a way that that the enemies in my life and in my dreams never did.

We both lay there for a moment, both breathing heavy as we stared at each other.

"What the hell?" Trent managed to gasp out when he stopped coughing.

"I don't..." I stared down at my hands. "I don't know. I thought I was... somewhere else."

He sat up, rubbing his throat. A deep red mark marred his skin, but he didn't seem upset. Instead, he looked at me with deep sorrow.

"Did you see visions as well?"

Visions?

Right. We were on a mission, following the path on Rose Milford's map, starting from the old mill, and going all the way to the secret mausoleum. I'd held a curtain of ivy aside for Trent to pass under a strange archway, but when I stepped through myself, I ended up lost on a battlefield from my memories.

"Yeah." I ran a shaky hand through my

hair, pushing the disheveled braid back over my shoulder. "Something like that. Are you all right?"

I reached for him, bracing one hand against the ground to haul myself onto my feet, but the moment I touched the dirt my whole hand sunk right up to my wrist.

"Fucking hell!"

No matter how hard I tugged, I couldn't pull it out. It felt as though something under the ground was holding onto me, pulling me farther under the surface.

Trent scrambled to grab my arm just below the elbow and started pulling as well. With the two of us combined, we managed to rescue my hand, but the moment I was free, both of our feet started sinking into the ground.

"What is this? Quicksand?"

I shook my head. "Quicksand doesn't act like this."

In a matter of moments, Trent was up to his knees, sinking faster the more he fought. I was a little luckier. Only one of my legs was sinking, while I had managed to find solid purchase with one foot on a tree root.

"Quick. The trees aren't affected. Get up onto that tree stump."

Trent managed to take a few laborious steps, windmilling his arms for balance, but it wasn't enough. He couldn't reach the tree stump, and he was quickly sinking deeper.

I had a choice to make. Climb up onto the tree stump myself or help him get to safety.

It wasn't even a choice.

Grabbing his arm, I threw all my weight into pulling him out of the sinking dirt and practically threw him toward the tree stump. The laws of momentum meant I went tumbling in the opposite direction, farther away from safety, but it was worth it when I saw his fingers dig into the crumbling bark.

With a squelching sound of wet mud, Trent pulled his feet free and climbed onto the safety of the tree stump. The sight of him, safe, was such a relief, I almost didn't notice as I sank all the way up to my waist.

"Magnus!" Trent shouted.

I was angled slightly away from him and couldn't turn to look in his direction, but something jabbed at my shoulder.

"Grab on."

It was a tree branch. Trent must have picked it up from the ground and was using it to cross the distance between us.

I grabbed on, and with a great heave, Trent pulled me out of the ground and onto the safety of the tree stump. There was barely enough room for the both of us, and we had to cling together to keep from falling off.

It was embarrassing, huddling for

safety like some helpless damsel, but what else could I do?

If it was a person that was threatening us, I could fight them, but I couldn't punch the ground.

I wrapped my arm around Trent's waist, pulling him flush against me to ensure he didn't fall off. "It's all right. It's just a hallucination. It'll pass."

"A hallucination?"

Standing so close together, I couldn't see his face, but I heard the incredulous tone in his question."

"Yes, a hallucination," I insisted. "What else would it be?"

"Well..." Trent's voice dipped downward, like it had suddenly stepped off the edge of a cliff, and I felt him fidget within the circle of my arms. "Aunt Missy did say that the Milford sisters were witches."

On instinct, I nearly stepped back to look him in the eye, and only his grip on my shoulders kept me from tumbling right off the tree stump.

"Don't tell me you believe in magic."

"I don't know." Trent threw his hands into the air in frustration, but quickly grabbed back onto me as we both wobbled to stay on the tree stump. "This doesn't seem like a hallucination. We're both experiencing it. And what's causing it? Hallucinations don't just happen for no reason."

My foot slipped off the tree stump, nearly sinking back into the ground. I shook off the clinging mud and found a better position to stand that didn't put either of us in danger.

"I don't know why this is happening, but the idea that we were somehow drugged without knowing is still more believable than witches and magic. This isn't a fairytale."

"Still doesn't explain why we're both experiencing it," Trent grumbled, but otherwise seemed to accept my explanation.

We stood there, plastered together as we looked around our situation. We were too far away to reach any other tree or rock. Our tree stump was an isolated island. Safe, but alone.

"So?" Trent said after a moment when nothing happened. "Any idea what we do now?"

I shrugged, careful not to move my shoulders too much so I didn't unbalance either of us. "Not much to do until this hallucination wears off. There's no telling how much we're seeing is actually real. We don't even know where we really are, so for now, we just need to stay put until whatever is causing this runs its course."

"But that could take forever. We don't know what's causing it, so for all we know, it could last for days. You expect us to just stand here that long?"

Speaking with someone I could feel but

couldn't look at was very unnerving. I was aware of every flinch and muscle twitch in Trent's body, but I was cut off from the most basic of facial expressions to know what he was thinking.

It left me hyper-analyzing every slight change in the tone of his voice and reading way too much into even the smallest shift in posture. He was clearly unhappy, but I had no way of knowing the strength of those emotions, or where they were directed.

Was he mad at me?

Himself?

The situation?

There was no way to know, so I was extra cautious with my words.

"If it takes too long, we can try to come up with another idea, but for now, this is our only option. A hallucination this strong probably can't be maintained for too long, so it should wear off sooner or later."

MAGNUS

I felt the vibrations as Trent muttered under his breath, but even this close, I couldn't understand what he was saying.

Not that I needed to hear him. His meaning was clear anyway.

I could make all the claims I wanted, but neither of us knew the answer for certain.

We stood in silence for a while, with only the noise of the forest to keep us entertained. At first, I didn't notice anything unusual, but as I continued to listen to the various noises, I realized that it all sounded too perfect.

It was like someone had recorded various sounds of nature and edited them together into the best way, with only the clearest bird songs and an ideal breeze that rustled the trees in a steady rhythm.

A frog croaked somewhere in the distance, and it was such a cliché sound that it could have been pulled right from a National Geographic documentary.

Nature was never so perfect.

Birds were interrupted mid-song. The wind changed direction. So many noises all at once would inevitably end up overlapping and interfering with each other.

The unnatural perfection made a shiver travel up my spine. Trent must have noticed it, too, for I felt a shudder travel through him.

"So," he said, clearly just to break the silence. "When you were hallucinating earlier, you were seeing something from your time in the military, right? You've never really talked about it, but it seemed like you were fighting something."

I sighed. "Yeah. It's not really something I talk about a lot. Not even with Brody and Creed. We all did a lot of stuff during our years of service. Some of it good. Some of it bad. Most of it somewhere in between."

There were so many things I could tell

him about, but most were stories he wouldn't want to hear.

Like the bystander child that had been killed by a stray bullet. Even after an investigation, we could never be sure exactly whose bullet it had been, so I never knew if the innocent blood was on my hands or not.

Then there was the time we were aiding a refugee camp, only to discover that it was a trap. One moment our unit was handing out rations, and the next we were under attack. I'd only survived that incident because our attackers had randomly chosen to shoot the man standing next to me first, giving me time to dive for cover.

I couldn't tell Trent about those things. Maybe someday, but not today.

"Don't worry about it," I said, and shrugged again. "Even my worst memories are old friends by now. They don't bother me anymore. What about you? What did your hallucination show you?"

It was an underhanded tactic, distracting Trent with his own hallucinations so he stopped focusing on mine, but it worked. He immediately tensed up, and even without seeing his face I knew his thoughts were suddenly a million miles away.

"It wasn't anything important," he sighed, trying and failing to sound nonchalant. "Just some stupid childhood stuff. Although, there was one thing."

I could practically hear his thoughts turning over in his head as he debated with himself.

If his brain was a computer, it would have been screeching like an old AOL dialup tone.

I chuckled to myself as I pictured it, then laughed even harder when I realized how old that reference made me seem.

No, I didn't *seem* old. I was over forty.

MAGNUS

By most people's standards, I was officially "over the hill."

"Stupid childhood stuff, huh? Anything you want to tell me about?"

"No, not that, but..."

Very carefully, Trent pulled back as far as he could, so he was almost looking me in the eye.

"Magnus, can I ask about the lingerie we found in your closet?"

The question shouldn't have startled me, but it did. I'd been hoping we could move past that little discovery without a discussion, but I could never be so lucky. Of course, Trent would have questions about that.

There was nowhere to go. I couldn't even put space between our bodies. Deflecting the question would be nearly impossible if Trent really wanted an answer.

"Um, like I said. It's not important. Just something I bought on a whim."

"For a prospective partner," Trent nodded. "Yeah, you said that."

I thought this answer would reassure him, but it only seemed to make him more upset.

I sighed, and my breath ruffled his dark hair. "It's not something I'm into wearing, and I don't actually care about my partner wearing that kind of stuff. I'm not going to ask you to do that."

For a moment, Trent forgot our precarious position and nearly stepped away from me. Only by grabbing him at the last second and pulling him securely into my arms, was I able to keep him safely on the tree stump.

Pressed against me, he muttered something against my chest. I had to ask him to repeat himself, so he raised his head just enough to free his mouth, but not enough to look me in the eye.

"Why not?"

"Huh?"

MAGNUS

Somewhere along the way, I'd apparently lost the plot of our conversation, but I wasn't sure where. I thought we'd been on the same page and that I was offering reassurance, but all I'd done was make it worse.

An emotional tear dripped from the corner of Trent's eye before he quickly wiped it away.

"Why wouldn't you ask me? You say it so certainly. Like asking me isn't even a possibility, but why not?"

"Uh? What?"

This was ridiculous. Trying to talk with someone while I couldn't see their entire face was only making things more complicated.

Bending my knees and shifting my weight, I managed to lower myself enough that I could look up into Trent's face.

The expressions I found there were much more intense than I expected.

"Do you..." For a moment I hesitated,

433

certain that I must have been reading him wrong.

But so what if I was wrong?

I'd made a fool of myself plenty of times in front of men who meant only half of what Trent meant to me.

What was the point of building such a strong resistance to personal embarrassment if I wasn't going to use that skill now that Trent needed me to take a chance and be brave?

"Do you want to wear the lingerie?"

"I don't know," Trent exploded, his hands flailing out to the sides to avoid hitting me. "I've never tried wearing such a thing. It'd be stupid. But if that's the kind of thing you want your partner to wear for you, then how could you ever be satisfied with someone like me?"

"Whoa, hold up. What are you talking about? Why would it be stupid?"

Trent gestured at himself from head to toe. "Look at me."

Since he'd offered the invitation, I let my gaze drag up and down his body. "Okay." Grabbing him by the belt, I pulled him closer so that our hips aligned as intimately as possible. "I've looked. Now what?"

Trent scoffed and laid his hands on my chest like he was about to push me away, but then stopped. "I'd look ridiculous in lingerie. I can never give you that, and... I don't want you to be unsatisfied with me."

The bird songs around us fell silent and the wind made no noise as it rustled the leaves in the trees, but I didn't notice the suddenly missing noise. The moment Trent brought up the idea of him wearing lingerie, the image was seared into my mind. I could see nothing else as my imagination ran wild.

"So, you'd actually wear it if I asked?"

"What?"

Trent trembled in my arms, and although I couldn't see his face very well, I could tell from the soft tone of his voice that he wasn't upset.

No, he trembled for a much more pleasant reason.

It hadn't seemed possible, but I managed to pull him even closer, so he could feel the unmistakable evidence of exactly how attractive I found the idea of him in lingerie.

"I didn't ask because I assumed you wouldn't want to. But if you do want to, then we can absolutely do that."

Trent's shaking intensified and he buried his face against my shoulder. "You don't mean that. I'll look so stupid. There's nothing feminine or pretty about me. It won't suit me at all."

"Hey," I shouted before he'd even finished talking. "Shut up. First of all, you're damn hot in anything you wear. Secondly, so what if you're not feminine? Who said lingerie is only for feminine people? Last I checked, there's no law that says masculine people can't like pretty things as well."

Although he didn't raise his face, I could feel the heat of Trent's blush through my shirt. It seared right into my skin, and it was a miracle his face didn't literally burst into flames.

"So, if I wore it, you'd really like it?"

Wrapping my arms around his shoulders, I pressed a kiss to the top of his head.

"I'd love it."

Just to make my point, I jerked my hips forward to emphasize the arousal already tenting my pants.

Trent was silent for a moment, but then he slumped and leaned more of his weight against me.

"Okay. But we'll need to get a bigger size. I don't think the set you had would fit me."

I laughed and pressed another kiss against his head. Just as I was about to tell him I'd gladly buy all the lingerie he wanted, the feel of something tugging on my foot interrupted me.

Looking down, I found the muddy ground engulfing my shoe.

At first, I thought I'd accidentally stepped off the tree stump and tried to pull my leg free.

It wouldn't come out. I was still standing firmly on the tree stump, but the ground itself had reached up to take hold of me and its grip was iron strong.

"Trent, run," I shouted, shoving him away from me as the very earth itself pulled me down.

"Run? Fuck off," Trent shouted at me as he stayed rooted by my side. "Don't be stupid. I'm not going anywhere."

He didn't let go of me. Of course he didn't. I didn't really expect him to abandon me but trying to keep him safe had just been second nature.

Together, the two of us tried to free my

leg, but it was useless. With each moment that passed, I was pulled deeper and deeper into the ground until both my legs had disappeared.

The ground reached up like grasping hands and clamped onto Trent as well. The smell of wet earth filled my nose as a wave of mud washed over me. It invaded my mouth. My ears. I was suddenly rendered mute and deaf as I watched Trent get pulled down with me.

The last thing I saw was his single free hand desperately reaching for me before I was pulled completely under the surface of the earth, and everything went black.

***

I sat up with a violent jolt, gasping to breathe as deeply as I could.

My lungs protested the mistreatment, and I immediately started coughing. I doubled over, gagging so hard I nearly threw up. It was several minutes before I could breathe without sending myself into another fit, and when I looked up, I found a cup of water in front of my face.

"Here," someone said, pushing the water closer to me. "Drink."

I grabbed the cup and gulped down the water before I even knew who offered it.

At that point, even poison would have been appreciated if it could get the taste of dirt out of my mouth.

But wait... my mouth was completely clean.

As I polished off the water, I realized that the taste and smell of dirt, which had been so overwhelming earlier, had disappeared.

"It really was a hallucination."

That statement shouldn't have surprised me. I'd told Trent the exact same thing. Yet, as I'd sunk down under the ground, it had felt so real that I couldn't help doubting myself.

Maybe magic really did exist.

No, that was just the leftover thoughts of delusion. Trent and I were fine. It had all been a hallucination, just as I'd thought, and now it was over.

"Wait. Trent."

I jumped to my feet, intending to immediately find him, but my legs shook and refused to hold my weight. I crashed back onto my ass and started coughing again.

"Here." Another cup of water was thrust in front of my face. "Trent's fine. He's right over there. Now drink some more. You need it."

My gaze found Trent over the rim of the glass. He was lying on a mat just a few feet away, completely unconscious but otherwise unharmed.

My relief was not a gentle sigh, but rather struck with the force of a bowling ball right to my chest.

With my immediate concern settled, I could finally dedicate brain power toward the rest of our situation.

We were inside a large tent, the kind meant for groups of people that left plenty of space inside. It was a lot fancier than the basic tent Trent and I had brought for our trip through the forest, but a tent was still a tent. We were still surrounded by thin canvas walls, and I could feel the ground below me, so I knew we were still in the forest.

Wherever we'd ended up, we hadn't gone far.

The glass of water still waited in front of me, patiently held out by an unknown hand. I followed the hand up the arm to see Deputy Hillard standing there offering me the drink.

"Don't glare at me like that," he said when he noticed me staring at him. "I found you wandering around the woods hallucinating. If I wanted to harm you, I would have just left you there."

Since I'd already drunk one glass of

water, there was no reason to reject the second. This time, I drank it slower, observing the other man as I processed my situation.

If Trent and I had been drugged, then Deputy Hillard would be one of the top people on my suspects list. He was the one who'd tried to break into Trent's shop, had apparently been snooping around the Milford sisters' mausoleum, and used his position of authority to demand we hand over Rose Milford's locket.

However, none of that matched his current laid-back attitude. He was acting as if we'd merely run into each other at the grocery store rather than being lost out in the woods.

Finishing off the second drink of water, I handed the glass back.

"What's going on?"

As he accepted the newly empty glass, my gaze caught on the gold ring sitting on his finger. It was an obviously masculine style, with a thick band and minimalistic lines, but just like Aunt Missy's ring, it bore a clear design of three very specific flowers woven together.

Pieces clicked together in my mind. I couldn't see the full picture yet, but I knew the shape of the answers I needed.

Deputy Hillard opened his mouth, but before he could say a word, I cut him off.

"Don't you dare say anything about witches or magic. I don't care what you believe. I don't subscribe to any of the nonsense."

For a moment, Deputy Hillard paused and studied me, but then he set the glass aside among a stack of supplies pushed to one side of the tent and sat on the ground across from me.

"I take it you know about the *Mothers of the Mountain*."

"Yeah. And I take it you're one of their believers."

He didn't even try to deny it and

simply nodded. "Many people in Emberwood are. My family was always one of their biggest supporters. That's why I had to get the locket back from you. It's one of our sacred objects, so to speak."

I could almost understand his reasoning. If the holy grail of *Joan of Arc*'s sword suddenly appeared, there would be many people willing to do anything to get their hands on it. Religious fanaticism wasn't something I personally believed in, but I'd seen firsthand how impactful it could be on more than one occasion.

"Is that why you stole the journal and the key, too? To keep them safe?"

A look of anguish came over Deputy Hillard's face, and I knew the answer before he even spoke.

"No. I don't know who took them. That's why it was even more important to retrieve the locket. I was hoping you hadn't managed to open it, but I realize now that was naive."

There were so many questions I wanted to ask, but at that moment Trent started to stir, and the conversation came to a halt as I helped him wake up. He was groggy and disoriented, groping out blindly even before he opened his eyes like he was trying to climb the air.

Or dig his way out from being buried alive.

It took a few minutes and several glasses of water for Trent to recover from the aftereffects of his hallucination, and even longer to explain to him where we were. I couldn't give him any specifics. Other than the fact that we were in a tent, I didn't know exactly where in the forest we'd ended up. There was no telling how long we'd been wandering around while stuck in our shared vision. We could have ended up miles off course.

Considering this, it was a miracle Deputy Hillard had managed to find us at all.

"I knew what to look for," he said when I asked him about how he located us. "As soon as I heard you'd gone out to the old mill, I knew that you were going to follow the path out to the mausoleum."

"But, we've been there before," Trent pointed out, his voice still groggy after waking up. "Why would it matter this time?"

"Because you followed that specific path."

Deputy Hillard pulled out the map that had been hidden in Rose Milford's locket. It was only a replica, the real one was probably locked away safe somewhere, but even written on modern printer paper, that path was unmistakable.

"It's not just the mausoleum that's important, but the path to get there," Deputy Hillard explained. "According to my family's history, when the *Mothers of the Mountain* appeared out of the forest, this is the exact path that they took to get here. It's a sojourn, of sorts. Meant to test the worthiness of the ones walking it. If you could make it to the sacred grotto, then you were worthy. Of course, that was back when the path was maintained. Now, left to grow wild, it's out of balance so its affect is unpredictable."

Deputy Hillard's word choice caught my attention. "Grow wild." A path didn't grow. It could crumble, or fall into decay, but it didn't grow.

A key piece of the puzzle clicked together in my mind.

"It's the plants."

Beside me, Trent looked confused by my sudden statement, but there was no surprise on Deputy Hillard's face.

I turned to Trent, mostly ignoring the Deputy as I explained.

"There was that strange plant I didn't recognize at the mausoleum. And when we were following the path from the mill, I noticed that the surrounding plants looked strange. I recognized them all, but something about them struck me as odd. I couldn't put my finger on what, exactly, was wrong, so I ignored it, but all the plants just seemed a little off somehow."

Although I hadn't been talking to him, or even asked him a question, Deputy Hillard answered me anyway.

"The *Mothers of the Mountain* each had their special skills. Rose Milford had a talent for plant life. The plants along that path were bred specifically by her, and she gave them unique properties that induce hallucinations. I've studied them for years and I still don't understand how she did it. Encountering one of her altered plants won't do anything, but being exposed to all the plants along that path in their exact order will... well, you experienced it for yourselves."

It was probably lucky that I'd experienced the effect of Rose Milford's plants for myself, or else I never would have believed him. It almost seemed otherworldly.

No. Certainly not. Magic didn't exist.

I simply didn't have enough knowledge to understand the logical answer.

As soon as I got home from this adventure, I vowed to do more research into plant breeding and the properties of hallucinogens.

"This all seems rather excessive," Trent pointed out, pulling me from my thoughts. "What's the point of it all?"

The ring on Deputy Hillard's finger flashed in the light as he nervously spun it in circles. He was lost in thought for a few moments, muttering under his breath as he debated with himself, and occasionally glancing up at us. After a few minutes of this, he seemed to come to a decision, and nodded to himself.

"You have been pulled into this, so I guess you deserve to know. All right. If you're willing to come with me, I'll show you the answer."

CHAPTER FOURTEEN

Trent

WHEN DEPUTY HILLARD said he would show us the answer, I expected to find something new.

Instead, he took us right back to the hidden mausoleum that we'd seen before.

It took several days for us to reach the mausoleum, and since Magnus and I had lost our supplies, we were forced to rely on Deputy Hillard. It was awkward sleeping in the tent with the man, but overall, it did at least help reassure us that Deputy Hillard was sincere in his intentions.

The mausoleum looked exactly the same as the last time we'd visited. Even the path through the thorny unidentifiable plants had started to grow back already, making the structure look as untouched as before.

Of course, Magnus was first drawn to the plant in question, prodding at it with a stick to once again uncover the doorway.

"Is this plant also one of Rose Milford's creations. I've tried looking it up, but I couldn't find anything."

"I assume so," Deputy Hillard said as he helped to clear the doorway. "I've done some research myself and also come up empty-handed, so I assume it's a new breed of plant that she bred on her own. It's particularly hardy, so I try not to mess with it other than when I come out here to check up on things and make sure no one's tampered with the place."

Since the newly grown plants weren't as deeply rooted as the older growth, they were much easier to move aside, and we soon had access to the mausoleum once again.

It was a lovely area, with a waterfall and the tranquil pond shielded by the high cliff. As I looked upon the three stone crypts, I could understand why someone would choose it as their final resting place. According to Deputy Milford, this had been the spot where the three sisters met with their most loyal followers—which only made it seem more like a religion—so the area had significance even before their death.

"Okay, so now what?" Magnus asked as he looked around the mausoleum. "We've seen this before, so what did we miss."

In response, Deputy Hillard just pointed at the three crypts.

"Anyone who doesn't follow the *Mothers of the Mountain* wouldn't know this, but they were very connected with the nature of the area. They never would have wanted their final resting place to be sealed away in stone boxes."

Taking the ring from his hand, he aligned the image of the three interwoven flowers with a hidden depression on the underside of the lid of Rose's coffin. A vibration passed through the floor before we heard a clicking sound of something out of sight falling into place.

With that done, he then braced his hands against the top of Rose's crypt and shoved. If it were a proper coffin, the lid wouldn't have moved aside so easily, but it slid with the efficiency of oiled hinges, revealing the space within.

There was no body. Instead, we were faced with a set of narrow stairs leading down into the earth.

"Are we seriously going down there?" I

asked Magnus, but Deputy Hillard was already climbing over the side of the crypt and heading down into the dark tunnel.

Magnus just shrugged at me. "I guess we are."

Whoever had constructed the underground stairs obviously hadn't been thinking about men like me. Deputy Hillard managed without too much trouble, but both Magnus and I were forced to duck and turn sideways to fit through the tunnel. Even then it was a tight squeeze. My front and back both dragged against the walls of the tunnel as I navigated the shallow steps, and I inevitably bumped my head several times along the way.

Our only saving grace was the fact that it wasn't a particularly long staircase. After only about twenty feet, it leveled out, and then after another fifty feet, it ended. Such a short distance that only took us a few minutes to cover, and yet the difference between one side of the tunnel and the other was astounding.

The tunnel opened up to what I could only call a "secret garden." About the size of a football field, the entire area was covered in so much color and greenery, it looked like a literal jungle. Everything grew wild, but there were still remnants of paths laid over the ground that made it clear everything had once been carefully planned out and planted with intent.

High cliff walls rose on every side of the garden, leaving only a small circle of sky open far above our heads. It would have been too dark in such an enclosed space to sustain so many plants, but large mirrors had been placed at strategic points around the garden to redirect the sunlight. Even the most hidden corners of the garden had plenty of sunlight.

I didn't know much about plants, but even I could recognize how much effort had gone into making sure that every plant in the entire place had exactly what it needed to thrive.

The sound of someone gasping beside me made me glance over at Magnus. He looked starstruck as he gazed around the secret garden, as if he'd suddenly found himself transported to heaven and struggled to take it all in at once.

"This is..."

He never finished the sentence as he wandered over to the nearest batch of flowers and started examining their setup.

It didn't matter. Sentences weren't needed. Even someone without a hint of a green thumb, like me, knew exactly what Magnus meant.

The garden was astounding.

"My family comes by every now and then to maintain the mirrors," Deputy Hillard explained as he idly toyed with a nearby fern leaf. "But other than that, we mostly leave the garden alone. A lot of the plants here can't be found anywhere else.

Some of them are uniquely bred creations, and some of them are extinct species that Rose Milford somehow managed to preserve. They're priceless."

There was no joy in his voice as he said this. Deputy Hillard wasn't bragging when he emphasized how rare the garden was.

He was warning us.

Over the course of history, many graves and monuments had been robbed by treasure hunters for the sake of money. Plants may not be as flashy as gold or jewels, but if they were rare then they were worth money, and if they were worth money, someone would inevitably try to take it for themselves.

It was the same reason I had such a complex security system on my antique shop. Deputy Hillard's late night visit wasn't the first time I'd dealt with someone trying to break in.

Magnus wasn't listening. He was too

busy exploring the plant life around us and marveling at the unique specimens.

To offer assurances, I held Deputy Hillard's eye for a moment and nodded.

"I can see why you've worked so hard to keep it secret. A place like this shouldn't be disturbed."

The tension drained from Deputy Hillard's face. He knew we'd keep the garden a secret, which seemed to be all he wanted in the end.

A part of me was curious about the other two sisters. If Rose Milford's crypt led to this majestic place, then what secrets could Lisianthus and Poppy Milford's crypts be hiding?

I kept those questions to myself. Deputy Hillard had gone to such lengths to preserve the secrets of this garden, and only revealed them when Magnus and I literally stumbled right into the thick of things. The man wasn't going to reveal anything more than necessary.

In the end, I decided I didn't need to know. Watching the joy in Magnus's eyes as he investigated the one-of-a-kind garden was enough for me. He was more excited than a child in Disney Land, muttering to himself and taking a dozen close-up pictures of every unique plant he found.

After hiking through the forest for several days my legs were tired. So, after a few minutes, I sat cross-legged directly on the ground and prepared myself for a long wait as I watched Magnus explore.

We were going to be here a while.

***

By the time we eventually returned from our trip, Brody had managed to finish a little more of Magnus's house. It still wasn't done, but there was a sitting area now, along with the bedroom, and even the beginning of a full kitchen. It was coming along. What was once just a skeleton of a house was slowly gaining pieces of a body, fleshing out the shape of a true home.

It was finally over. We'd found the likely identity of the body that Magnus unearthed and figured out why Deputy Hillard tried to break into my shop. We didn't even have Rose's locket anymore.

Some questions were still unanswered, like what was behind the coffee beans hidden in Rose's locket, and who stole the journal and key which had also been found in the coffin.

However, these questions didn't concern us. Our role in the story was done. We could move on and leave it to more qualified people to find the rest of these answers.

After getting back home—and reassuring Deputy Hillard several more times that we wouldn't tell anyone about the mausoleum or the secret garden— Magnus and I were too tired to do anything but sleep. Several days passed, where our biggest worry was what to have for lunch, and if the weather would allow Magnus to finally start constructing the greenhouse he wanted.

These days of leisure were probably at fault for my sudden fit of madness. We'd been so busy for so long that I wasn't used to not having anything to worry about. Because of that, I couldn't help thinking back on everything I'd experienced in my hallucination. Those memories replayed over and over in my mind, until eventually, I decided to do something about it.

I almost immediately regretted that decision.

"This was a bad idea," I mumbled under my breath as I looked at myself in the mirror.

In a moment of insanity, I'd bought a set of lingerie for myself. It was surprisingly easy. One could really find anything online, and express overnight shipping meant I didn't even have to wait long for the package to turn up at my doorstep.

Now, I stood in Magnus's bathroom, glaring at my own reflection.

As I'd suspected, the lingerie that Magnus had bought was too small for me, plus the bright blue color didn't match my taste. The set that I'd bought not only fit me, but was a more understated black. The only hint of color on the whole outfit was the laces on the corset style top, which had looked red in the picture online, but in real life were actually pink. I'd hoped that this particular style of top would hide my body and force me into a more ideal shape, but it only seemed to emphasize my stomach more. My thighs spilled out of the tops of the fishnet stockings, threatening to rip right through the delicate fabric, and reminding me of the fact that this type of clothing was not made for people with my body type.

It was made for people with slender limbs, flat stomachs, and smooth skin. Not bulky weightlifters with plenty of both muscle and fat, and a thick smattering of body hair.

"This was so dumb," I griped while searching for a way to undo the corset. "Why did I think this would work?"

The corset laced up in the front and back, but the front laces were built in. Only the ones in the back could actually be untied. Getting into the thing had been difficult, but somehow getting out of it was even harder. I had to arch my back to get my arms behind me, but even then, I couldn't find the end of the string.

The bathroom door suddenly opened.

"Hey, Trent, I—" Magnus stepped through the bathroom doorway and we both froze.

"I can explain," I quickly said, but then fell silent.

What could I realistically say that would explain why I was arched over the bathroom sink with one hand braced on the mirror, practically sticking my ass in the air while dressed in something fit for a strip club?

"Explain?" Magnus stared wide-eyed at me, not moving a muscle. "Yeah, you definitely need to explain why you didn't warn me about this. There were things I wanted to get done today, but now none of that's happening."

He came toward me, hands outstretched, and I backed away.

"Sorry. I know it's bad. I'm taking it off."

Magnus froze again, looking even more shocked than he had when he first opened the door.

"What? Sorry? Why? What do you mean?"

The damn string to the corset still eluded me, so I started tugging at the top of one of my stockings, but they clung to me so tightly that the fabric didn't want to budge.

"Sorry about this. It was a bad idea. I shouldn't have even put this thing on."

Magnus clasped mt hands in a soft grip and pulled them away from the uncooperative fabric. "Does this have to do with what we talked about earlier? I know we were hallucinating at them time, so maybe I'm remembering it wrong, but I thought I told you that I'd love to see you in something like this."

"Yeah, but that was before seeing..." I gestured angrily down at my body. "I mean, look at me."

"I am." He gripped my hips and pulled me closer. "I could spend all day looking at you like this."

"You don't mean..." I bit my lip and looked away from him, unable to meet his eye. "You can't actually like the way I look in this."

"You don't believe me? Here. I'll show you."

He grabbed one of my hands and pressed it between his legs. There was no denying the hardness I felt under my palm. It was clear as day, even through the thick fabric of his jeans.

"Convinced yet? I really do find you hot. Insanely hot. So much so, that I'm having trouble thinking straight right now."

He stepped forward, pressing my back until my mostly bare ass hit the edge of the sink. Each of his hands braced against the counter, caging me in as he leaned closer to whisper directly into my ear.

"Now, tell me. Do you like wearing this? There's no point if you don't like it. But I think you do, otherwise you wouldn't have put it on in the first place."

Swallowing hard, I slid my palms down the front of the corset, admiring the feel of lace and leather.

"I think... I like the idea of it. I like feeling sexy and desirable. I even like being pretty sometimes. I just... didn't think I could."

"You definitely can." He attacked my neck with his lips, sucking and licking along my skin all the way from ear to collarbone. "Please keep it on. I'll buy you a hundred of them. You'll never have to wear anything else if you don't want to."

I laughed and wrapped my arms around his shoulders. "That's a bit excessive. Let's just stick to one outfit for now."

His arousal pressed up against me, and my own blood began to heat up in response. I wasn't hard yet, but I was quickly getting there.

I ran one of my hands through his long hair, which was currently unbound, and I nipped at the shell of his ear.

"If you really do like the look of me in

this, then prove it."

Magnus didn't need to be told twice. The moment those words left my lips, he immediately grabbed my waist and spun me around so I was facing the mirror. I was thrown off by the unexpected sight of myself, which I was still getting used to, but any awkwardness I felt vanished when I saw the genuine heat in Magnus's eyes.

He took a moment to search through the bathroom drawers and pulled out some condoms and lubricant, which he tossed onto the counter.

"Tomorrow, we are making appointments to get tested. I'm tired of using these things."

I could do nothing but nod as he squeezed my ass in his large hand and stole my voice right out of my throat. He pulled the bottoms of the lingerie down just far enough to expose me and left everything else in place. Already my knees were trembling and we'd barely done anything. I was going to be nothing but a puddle on the floor by the time we were done.

After fumbling with the lube for a moment, Magnus slid his fingers down the cleft of my ass and one digit slowly pushed inside me. With the bottom half of the lingerie still clinging to my thighs, I couldn't spread my legs very far apart. Even with the aid of lube, it felt tighter than usual as his fingers stretched me open.

Arousal burned hot in my gut now, and I shouted when he brushed that most sensitive spot inside me.

This wasn't going to take very long.

The countertop was cool under my skin as I braced my forearms against it, which left me slightly bent over. My nose was only inches from the mirror. I was already panting, and my breath fogged up the glass, blurring the reflection of myself.

MAGNUS

One finger quickly became two, then three. Soon enough, Magnus was plunging his fingers in and out of me, filling the bathroom with wet, squelching sounds as he thoroughly spread the lube around my inner walls.

"Hurry up," I gasped and thrust my hips backward to get him deeper. "I'm ready. Stop teasing me and get on with it."

"So impatient," Magnus grumbled, but he pulled his fingers out of me, and a moment later, I heard the sound of a zipper being pulled down and a condom package being torn open.

When Magnus finally pressed inside me, my whole body shook, and I had to brace one hand against the mirror to keep from completely collapsing. At first, his movements were slow and gentle, carefully waiting for me to adjust to his intrusion. It reminded me of a lukewarm bath. Pleasant, but not intense enough to be pleasurable.

Once he was all the way inside, however, that gentleness flew right out the window. His fingers gripped my hips hard enough to bruise as he pulled out and slammed right back in, managing to hit all my best spots at once. Lightning erupted across my nervous system, and all my thoughts turned to white noise as he fucked me hard and rough. Magnus panted directly into my ear, singing my praises with each thrust, but I couldn't hear it over the sound of my own racing heartbeat.

Items crashed to the floor as they were knocked off the bathroom counter. My bare feet slid on the tile and I struggled to find traction. In this position, I could barely move as Magnus pressed his pressed down on me, jolting my whole body each time he plunged back inside.

Tighter and tighter the pleasure coiled in my stomach. I clawed my nails helplessly at the smooth surface of the mirror, leaving streaks in the condensation of my own breath.

I was probably shouting, though I couldn't be sure. The whole world flipped inside out as I raced toward the edge of my own completion.

Each thrust seemed to come harder and faster, until everything blurred together into an unending ecstasy. Magnus wrapped one of his hands around me, sliding between my legs to stroke me in the same relentless rhythm as his thrusts. It was too much, and I came undone in his arms. My shouts echoed off the bathroom walls as every muscle in my body locked up.

The orgasm hit me in waves, one after the other, and Magnus's thrusts never slowed. He fucked me right through our shared climax, holding me tight until the pleasure finally began to abate and I was able to breathe freely once again.

We stayed that way for a few moments, catching our breath even as we remained tangled together. Magnus pressed idle kisses along my shoulders and slid his hands up and down my sides like he was trying to calm a wild animal.

"That was..." His voice trailed off, as he was clearly unable to think of the right words.

I sat up so I was no longer bent completely over the counter, letting my back press against his chest.

"If you're going to be that vigorous every time I wear something like this, we'll have to save it only for special occasions. I don't think I'll be moving for the rest of the day."

Magnus bit the lobe of my ear, and I could tell he was about to say something, but he was interrupted by an unexpected knock at the door.

"Magnus," Brody shouted. "Get out here."

MAGNUS

He was so loud that, although he was standing outside the house, it sounded like he was banging directly on the bathroom door.

Magnus turned away from me just enough to avoid screaming directly in my ear and called back, "I'm busy, Brody. Fuck off."

"I don't care," Brody shouted back. "Put your dick back in your pants and get your ass out here. I need to talk to you."

Heaving a heavy sigh, Magnus pulled himself off of me. "Even with my own house, I can't get five minutes of privacy."

We cleaned up as quickly as we could. There was no time to extract me from the complicated lingerie set, so Magnus gave me a long bathrobe to wear over it. The robe went all the way down to my ankles, so my legs would be covered.

Hopefully, Brody wouldn't look at my feet, where my stockings were still visible.

I clutched the front of the robe high up

against my throat as Magnus opened the front door.

"Damn, Brody. Calm down. What? Is the world ending?"

Brody glared at Magnus but didn't react to the sarcastic comment.

"I just got a call from the police department with information about the body we discovered."

"Yeah," Magnus shrugged and leaned against the doorframe, coincidentally blocking most of me from Brody's line of sight. "So what? We already figured out that the body was Jacob Thornley. The guy went missing after repeatedly harassing the Milford family and trying to get the sisters thrown out of town. It doesn't take a genius to put two and two together."

"Well, apparently it does. Jacob Thornley was in his sixties when he disappeared. But apparently the body that we found was only in its early forties when that person died. So, unless Jacob Thornley is a time traveler, he isn't the one who was buried in our ground."

Magnus and I shared a look, both of us clearly thinking the same thing.

My hands fell away from where they were gripping my robe closed. I no longer cared if Brody noticed what I was wearing underneath the robe. We had much bigger problems waiting for us.

It wasn't over. Not by a long shot.

Click now to read *Brody*, the next book in the Rock Hard Mountain Men series.

Dear Reader,

THANK YOU for reading Magnus, book one in the Rock Hard Mountain Men series.

If you enjoyed this taste of brawny, hairy alpha men who once lived to serve their country, and now strive for nothing more than a simple life with some peace and quiet—yet seem to attract action and mystery, and perhaps a little bit of man on man lovin' along the way, then please let me know.

You can simply return to the online retailer where you made your purchase and leave me a short review.

Your thoughts may just encourage other readers to try my books, and help me continue writing the characters we all adore and root for.

Even a few words would mean the world to me.

☺

~Love, Evie Riley

OTHER BOOKS BY EVIE

My action-filled, romantic suspense, and darker-themed books:

Rock Hard Mountain Men
Magnus
Brody
Creed

Ruthless Empire
Courting Danger
Chasing Danger
Kissing Danger

Federal Protection Agency
Mason
Rafe
Ryzen
Cooper
Noah
Damien
Sebastian

My more romance-themed books:

Rock His World

Hollow Heart

Wild Stars

Grave Misgivings

Jasper Springs

Cade

Dawson

Drew

Grayson

Riley

Mitch

ABOUT THE AUTHOR

Evie Riley believes too much time spent at the beach is barely enough. She enjoys spending time puttering in the garden, cooking yummy things for her family, and has a quirky personality, described by her partner as ranging from cute to deadly, depending on her blood-chocolate levels.

Evie crafts steamy gay male romance filled with all the edgy angst, or dark and gritty romantic suspense where her men must overcome difficult obstacles and may find love along the way while dishing out their own brand of justice.

Evie spends her nights writing bad boys in love, and her days wrangling the sweet boys she loves.

EVIE RILEY